The Art

The Art of Good Bidding

TERENCE REESE
and
DAVID BIRD

faber and faber
LONDON · BOSTON

First published in 1992
by Faber and Faber Limited
3 Queen Square London WC1N 3AU

Photoset by Parker Typesetting Service, Leicester
Printed in England by Clays Ltd, St Ives plc

Terence Reese and David Bird are hereby identified as authors
of this work in accordance with Section 77 of the Copyright,
Designs and Patents Act 1988

A CIP record for this book is available from the British Library

ISBN 0–571–16716–0

2 4 6 8 10 9 7 5 3

Contents

Introduction

At rubber bridge the contestants face each other relatively unarmed, as far as conventions are concerned. Does this mean that their bidding is inaccurate? Certainly not at the top level. If you took an hour or so of your time to watch any high-stake table at a London or New York card club you would be surprised at what can be achieved while playing only the most basic of conventions.

In tournament bridge the situation is different. Players load their convention cards to the limit, searching for any small advantage that can be gained.

In this book we explain how to bid well in either of the two bridge battlefields. Most of the text is concerned with good, convention-free, bidding. Each chapter, though, is studded with the best of the conventions popular in tournament play. These are assessed on a star system – 3-star conventions are rated as an essential part of your weaponry, 2-star conventions offer a considerable advantage and should be on the card of any aspiring tournament pair, 1-star conventions are more specialized and are of interest, perhaps, only to regular partnerships.

Terence Reese
David Bird

Opening on Balanced Hands

'Now, what sort of notrump do you like?'

This is the traditional first question when you play with someone for the first time. There are three basic answers: weak throughout, strong throughout, or variable. You may have a preference already for one of these three. Even so, you will need to adjust to different partners. Each method has its good and bad points and we will look at these in turn.

Weak (12–14) notrump throughout

One advantage of this method is its simplicity. You open 1 NT on virtually all flat hands in the 12–14 range. When you hold more than 14 points you will be strong enough to rebid 2 NT, facing a two-level response. This means you can open on any 4-card suit, without fear of having no sound rebid.

Since an opening 1 NT is such a descriptive call and is relatively dangerous to overcall, it is an advantage if you can make the call as often as possible. That is a second advantage of the weak notrump; hands in the 12–14 range are twice as frequent as those containing 15–17 points.

The main disadvantage of the weak notrump, particularly when you are vulnerable, is that every now and again you will suffer a large penalty. This is acceptable at pairs, where several small gains outweigh one big loss. At rubber bridge or teams, though, playing a weak notrump vulnerable is a dangerous business. Nevertheless there are many players who favour 'weak throughout' (mostly in Britain, it's true).

Strong (15–17) notrump throughout

By strengthening the requirement for an opening 1 NT you greatly reduce the risk of being doubled and conceding a large penalty. Also, it is dangerous to compete against a strong notrump; you will usually have the auction to yourselves.

A disadvantage of the strong notrump is that you sometimes have to open a 'prepared club' on hands in the 12–14 range (we will look at that later).

'Strong throughout' is the most popular scheme worldwide, favoured by nearly all Continental and US players.

Variable notrump

In traditional Acol 1 NT shows 12–14 when non-vulnerable, 15–17 when vulnerable. This is a safe and satisfactory method for rubber bridge or team play and to some extent gives you the best of both worlds. In pairs the tendency is towards weak throughout, or weak except when vulnerable against non-vulnerable.

The 1 NT rebid

In all cases the 1 NT rebid shows the opposite strength to that of a 1 NT opening. So, if you play a 12–14 notrump a 1 NT rebid shows 15–16 (not 17, note); if you play a 15–17 notrump, a 1 NT rebid shows 12–14.

Let's look at some typical flat hands and see how you would open them, depending on whether you are playing the weak or strong notrump.

(1) ♠ A Q 9 2 ♡ K 10 4 ♢ 7 2 ♣ A J 5 4

Fine for a weak notrump; you need not be deterred by the small doubleton. It is a mistake to open 1♣ instead, intending to rebid 1♠; you misdescribe the nature of your hand and allow the opponents an easy entry into the auction.

Playing a strong notrump, you start with 1♣. If partner responds 1◇ you rebid 1 NT; if instead he responds 1♡ or 1♠ you can give him a single raise.

(2) ♠ K J 7 4 ♡ A Q 8 3 ◇ 10 4 ♣ K 5 2

Again no problem if you play a weak notrump. Playing 15–17, start with 1♣ intending to rebid 1 NT over 1◇. Some players prefer to open 1♠ and rebid 2♡, but this is all too likely to end in a poor 2♠ contract on a 4–3 or even a 4–2 fit.

(3) ♠ A 3 ♡ Q 10 4 ◇ K 10 5 4 2 ♣ K 7 3

Playing weak, you are happy to open 1 NT; a 5-card minor is an acceptable and welcome feature of any notrump opening. Playing strong, you start with 1◇. You can rebid 1 NT over 1♠, raise 1♡ to 2♡ and repeat the diamonds over 2♣.

(4) ♠ K 10 5 ♡ A Q J 3 ◇ J 4 ♣ A J 10 2

This is too strong for a weak notrump, so you must bid a suit with the intention of rebidding in notrumps. Since you are strong enough to rebid 2 NT facing a two-level response, it is better to open 1♡, showing the major. Playing a strong notrump, you have a choice of calls. If you're willing to tolerate the weak doubleton in diamonds you can start with 1 NT. Alternatively you can start with 1♡ (the sequence 1♡–2◇–2 NT shows 15–16, whatever opening 1 NT you play).

(5) ♠ 10 8 7 4 ♡ K J 4 ◇ A Q 4 ♣ A Q 3

It is not attractive to open 1♠ on four to the 10 (although some players would!), so followers of the weak notrump must start with 1♣. No problem for the strong-notrumpers, of course.

There is one type of hand that is very awkward for those who favour the strong notrump:

(6) ♠ Q 9 7 6 ♡ A Q 8 4 ◇ Q 10 3 ♣ K 4

You cannot open 1◇ or 1♡ because that would leave you with no rebid over 2♣ (2 NT would promise 15–16, remember). You could, at a pinch, open 1♠ and rebid 2♡. That is hardly attractive on such poor spades, though. We cannot offer any happy solution.

Flat hands of 17–18 points

A jump rebid in notrumps indicates about 17 or 18 points, whatever range of 1 NT opening you are playing. These are typical hands:

(7)   ♠ K Q 9 2   ♡ A J 8 4   ◇ K J 2   ♣ A 5

Open 1♡. Partner has the chance to introduce spades. If instead he responds two of a minor, you rebid 3 NT.

(8)   ♠ K 10 8 4   ♡ A Q 4   ◇ K 5   ♣ A Q 9 4

Open 1♣, intending to rebid 2 NT over a response in either red suit.

Flat hands of 19 (sometimes 20) points

Hands of 19 points, not quite enough to open 2 NT, may be shown by a double-jump rebid of 3 NT.

(9)   ♠ A K 5   ♡ K J 8   ◇ A J 6 5   ♣ Q J 6

Open 1◇ and rebid 3 NT over 1♡ or 1♠. Over 2♣, promising fair values, you would be a trifle strong for 3 NT. It would be safe enough to invent a bid such as 2♡ or 2♠; you would be able to deal with any continuation.

Flat hands of 20–22 points

Here we enter the realm of the 2 NT opening.

(10) ♠ A Q 9 5 2 ♡ K 9 5 ◇ A Q ♣ A Q 6

The only call is 2 NT. You are too strong for 1♠, and 2♠ (strong) would leave you with no sensible rebid over a 2 NT negative response.

(11) ♠ A K 10 ♡ A Q 9 2 ◇ A K 8 3 ♣ J 7

You may not like to open 2 NT with this indifferent club holding but there is no better call available.

Flat hands of 23 points or more

Nothing special to report here; you simply use one of these sequences:

2♣–2◇–2 NT	23–24 points
2♣–2◇–3 NT	25–27 points
2♣–2◇–4 NT	28–30 points

Not that the last one ever happens!

Opening on Unbalanced Hands

We will start by looking at some borderline opening hands. The first question to be answered is: does the hand merit an opening bid?

    (1)   ♠ K Q 10 8 7 4   ♡ 5   ◇ A J 6 3   ♣ 9 2

Open 1♠ at any score. Only 10 points, it's true, but you have a strong suit. Even better, the suit is spades, which are difficult to overcall. Another good feature of the hand is that your high cards coincide with your length, always an advantage.

    (2)   ♠ K 10 8 7 4   ♡ Q 5   ◇ A J 6 3   ♣ 9 2

The same hand as in (1) except that ♠Q has become ♡Q. And what a difference! This is not at all a sound opening in the first or second seat. In the third seat, where you don't need to prepare a rebid, an obstructive 1♠ would be in order.

    (3)   ♠ K Q 10 9 5   ♡ 10 7   ◇ A 6 3   ♣ 7 4 3

Here you are well short of an opening bid. Only in the third seat, non-vulnerable, should you open 1♠, aiming among other things to make life awkward for the player on your left.

    (4)   ♠ 4   ♡ K 6 2   ◇ Q 10 7 3 2   ♣ A K 6 2

Here you have the values to open and would normally bid 1◇. In the fourth seat, though, it is wiser to pass. If you open you give the opposition a second chance to find their likely spade fit.

Deciding which suit to open

There are some useful general rules on the choice of suit to open. With two 5-card suits you generally open the higher suit (except on some hands with spades and clubs). With 5–4 shape you normally call the longer suit first.

Here are some 5–5 hands where the best opening call may be in doubt:

(5)   ♠ A 4   ♡ J 9 7 6 3   ◇ A K J 5 2   ♣ 6

Open 1♡. If you open 1◇ (because the suit is stronger) it will not be easy to convey that you hold five hearts as well; also, if partner holds the same length in the two suits it will be better to play with the *weaker* suit as trumps.

(6)   ♠ K 10 8 5 3   ♡ A 5   ◇ 4   ♣ A Q 8 6 3

Open 1♣, the normal bid with 5–5 in the black suits. You may have the opportunity to bid spades twice, so indicating your 5–5 shape.

(7)   ♠ A Q J 7 4   ♡ 3   ◇ K 6   ♣ Q 10 6 4 2

Open 1♠. It would not be a mistake to open 1♣, but the spades are fairly strong and you would not welcome competition in the red suits. If partner responds two of a red suit himself you will rebid 2♠ (a 3♣ rebid would indicate a stronger hand, as we will see later).

With 5–4 shape you normally show the longer suit first.

(8)   ♠ A K J 5   ♡ K 6   ◇ Q 9 7 4 2   ♣ 5 3

Open 1◇. Start with the 5-card suit. If partner responds 2♣, you will rebid 2◇ (again the apparent alternative, 2♠, would show a stronger hand).

(9)   ♠ K 6   ♡ A K J 5   ◇ Q 9 7 4 2   ♣ 5 3

Swap the majors round and we have one of the few hands where

7

you should open the 4-card suit. Open 1♡. The suits are touching and the hearts are packed with high cards. You plan to rebid 2◇ and won't mind ending in 2♡ on a 4–3 fit.

(10)   ♠ 6 3   ♡ K Q 6 2   ◇ A J 9 7 4   ♣ Q 5

Here you open 1◇. The hearts are weaker and a 2♡ contract on K Q x x opposite x x x would not be welcome. Nor would you fancy a sequence such as 1♡–2♣, 2◇–3♡.

(11)   ♠ A 4 3   ♡ A Q J 4   ◇ K Q 8 5 2   ♣ 9

Now you are strong enough to open 1◇ and rebid 2♡; there is consequently no need to bid the suits in an unnatural order. Such a sequence, where you rebid at the two-level in a suit higher than the one you opened, is known as a 'reverse' and suggests at least 16 points.

Opening on 4–4–4–1 hands

There is no need to remember special 'rules' here. Just check that you will have a descriptive and sound rebid available if partner responds in your short suit. Bearing that in mind, what would you open on these hands?

(12)   ♠ A 10 8 5   ♡ K J 6 3   ◇ 4   ♣ A 9 6 2

Start with 1♣. Over 1◇ you will rebid 1♡.

(13)   ♠ A K 9 3   ♡ 4   ◇ K Q 9 4   ♣ 10 7 5 2

Open 1◇, showing the better minor. Switch the minors and you would open 1♣.

(14)   ♠ 5   ♡ A K 10 6   ◇ K J 5 3   ♣ J 9 7 6

Here you start with 1♡. If partner says 1♠, there is not much to choose between various rebids on the next round.

When you are strong

On powerful distributional hands you must decide whether to open with a one-bid, a (strong) two-bid, or a 2♣ call.

Choose a one-bid when game is unlikely unless partner has enough to respond at the one-level. Open with a two-bid on a hand of power and quality, containing either one or two suits. On one-suited hands a strong two-bid will usually contain eight or more playing tricks. The 2♣ opening is used on balanced hands of 23 points or more, also on unbalanced hands that are rich in controls and worthy of a game contract in their own right.

What opening bid would you choose on these desirable holdings?

(15) ♠ A Q 8 5 2   ♡ A Q 7 2   ◇ A 10   ♣ K 6

Here you open 1♠. You have a fine hand, certainly, but if partner cannot find a response to 1♠, game is unlikely.

(16) ♠ A K J 10 7 2   ♡ 8   ◇ A 5   ♣ A J 9 2

Now you're worth a 2♠ opening. A card such as ♣K would be enough to give you a play for game, so you would be apprehensive if you opened 1♠ and this were passed out.

(17) ♠ A Q 10 2   ♡ A 2   ◇ 8   ♣ A K J 9 6 2

Start with 1♣. This hand is better in a way than the previous one and would be worth a two-bid if the main suit were not clubs. Still, there is little risk in a 1♣ opening; someone will surely speak.

(18) ♠ A Q 7   ♡ A J 8 3 2   ◇ A K   ♣ K Q 9

We are into 2♣ territory. Here you plan to rebid 2NT (non-forcing) over a negative 2◇ response. To rebid 2♡, forcing the auction to game, would take you too high when partner had a bust.

(19) ♠ K Q J 10 8 2 ♥ A Q J 9 6 ♦ – ♣ A 8

Start with 2♠ on this one. You will end in game, at least, but the hand is unsuitable for a 2♣ opening; on so unbalanced a type you want to start naming your suits at once. If partner gives a negative 2 NT response to 2♠ you will rebid 3♥, still forcing.

3

The Concept of Limit Bids

During an auction you will sometimes be concerned to give a picture of your distribution and sometimes to express your strength and the limit of your ambitions. Bids that introduce a new suit are generally aimed at the first of these objectives and give no precise picture as to your strength. For example, a 1♡ opening might be based on a hand of 10 or 20 points; similarly, a 1♠ response might contain 6 or 20 points. Such bids are largely exploratory in nature.

When a bid defines the strength of your hand within fairly narrow limits, it is known as a limit bid. Most notrump bids, such as those underlined in the sequences below, are limit bids:

(1)	<u>1 NT</u>	<u>2 NT</u>
(2)	1♢	1♠
	<u>1 NT</u>	
(3)	1♡	<u>1 NT</u>
(4)	1♢	1♡
	1♠	<u>2 NT</u>

Another type of limit bid occurs when a suit is raised or repeated below game level:

(5)	1♡	<u>2♡ or 3♡</u>
(6)	1◇ <u>2◇ or 3◇</u>	1♠
(7)	1♡ <u>2♠ or 3♠</u>	1♠
(8)	1♣ 1♠	1♡ <u>2♠ or 3♠</u>

In nearly all auctions one player makes a limit bid at some stage and the other is then able to assess the level at which the contract should be played – part score, game or slam.

Look for the limit bid in these typical auctions:

West	East
♠ A Q 10 8 5	♠ J 2
♡ K J 4 3	♡ 10 8
◇ A 8	◇ K 10 5 4
♣ 7 5	♣ A Q J 9 2

West	East
1♠	2♣
2♡	2 NT
3 NT	End

The first three bids are exploratory, looking for a trump fit. None of these calls give an accurate picture of the bidder's strength. East then bids 2 NT, a limit bid that indicates around 10–12 points. The call is non-forcing, like all limit bids, but West has a healthy 14-count and can therefore tell that his side has around 25 points – enough for a shot at game.

West	East
♠ K 10 8 4	♠ Q J 7 2
♡ J 3	♡ A 9 4
◇ A Q 10 5 2	◇ 9 6 3
♣ K 5	♣ Q 8 2

West	East
1◇	1♠
2♠	End

West's rebid of just 2♠ indicates a minimum hand, so East passes. Had West's ♡J been ♡K he would have rebid 3♠, showing a better hand. East's values would then have justified a raise to game.

It is the essence of good bidding to limit your hand as soon as possible. As the bidding proceeds, your partner will not, or at any rate should not, forget your previous limit bid.

4

Responding to 1 NT and 2 NT

In this chapter we look at two schemes for responding to 1 NT. The first uses natural responses, as is traditional in rubber bridge. The second uses transfer responses, a method that is almost universal in tournament bridge.

We start by looking at perhaps the most famous of all bidding conventions, one that is applicable whether or not you use transfers.

3-star convention: Stayman

In the Stayman convention (do we need to tell you?) a 2♣ response to 1 NT asks whether the opener has a 4-card major. The opener rebids:

2♢	No 4–card major
2♡	four ♡, and maybe four ♠
2♠	four ♠, but not four ♡

No strength is promised by invoking Stayman; the auction may stop at the 2-level or head towards a slam. The Stayman bidder has various options on the next round of bidding:

2 of a major	sign–off
2 NT	limit bid
single raise of major	limit bid
3 of new suit	limit bid

These are typical Stayman sequences (we assume a weak no-trump but the sequences have the same meaning opposite a strong notrump):

West	East
♠ A Q 2	♠ K 10 5 2
♡ K 10 4 3	♡ J 8 6 2
♢ A 9 4	♢ Q 10 6 2
♣ J 7 2	♣ 5

West	East
1 NT	2♣
2♡	End

Searching for a safer spot than 1 NT, East intends to pass any response to his Stayman call.

West	East
♠ K Q 7 2	♠ A J 9 5
♡ A 4	♡ K 10 8
♢ 9 8 3	♢ J 10 5 2
♣ K 8 5 4	♣ Q 3

West	East
1 NT	2 ♣
2 ♠	3 ♠
End	

East raises to 3♠, inviting game. West, with just 12 points, declines. Had West rebid 2♢ or 2♡, East would have bid 2 NT at his second turn.

West	East
♠ A 10 5 4	♠ K Q 6 2
♡ K J 6 3	♡ Q 10 9
♢ Q 10 5	♢ K 9 7 3
♣ Q 8	♣ A 6

West	East
1 NT	2 ♣
2 ♡	3 NT
4 ♠	End

Since East did not bid 3 NT on the first round West correctly deduces that East must hold 4♠.

Natural responses to 1 NT

If you don't play transfers, this is the normal scheme of responses to 1 NT:

2 ♣	Stayman
2 ♢, 2 ♡, 2 ♠	Sign-off (also called a 'weak take-out')
2 NT	limit bid
3 any	game-forcing on a suit of 5 cards or more
3 NT, 4 ♡, 4 ♠	all game bids are to play
4 NT	limit bid

Let's look at some sequences (again a 12–14 1 NT is assumed):

West	East
♠ A Q 9 4	♠ 10 8 7 6 2
♡ 8 3	♡ Q 9 2
♢ K 10 2	♢ 9 7 6 5
♣ A J 5 4	♣ Q

West	East
1 NT	2 ♠
End	

West has an excellent spade fit and a maximum 1 NT but partner's sign-off should normally be respected.

West	East
♠ A J 9 4	♠ 3
♡ A 8 4	♡ K Q 7 2
◇ K 10 7 3	◇ Q 8 4
♣ 10 4	♣ A Q J 7 3

West	East
1 NT	3 ♣
3 ◇	3 ♡
3 NT	End

East shows a game-forcing hand with four hearts and at least five clubs. West, with no fit and secure guards in the unbid suits, settles for 3 NT.

3-star convention: transfer responses to 1 NT

A different, and better, scheme of responses to 1 NT involves the use of transfer bids. For example, a response of 2◇ indicates at least five hearts; partner will rebid 2♡ and you can then either pass or describe your hand further. All responses between 2◇ and 2 NT are conventional and we will look at them in turn.

The 2◇ transfer

A 2◇ response indicates at least five hearts. Unless the opener has exceptional support for this suit, he will rebid 2♡:

West	East
1 NT	2 ◇
2 ♡	?

The responder now has various options:

Pass	when he has no expectation of game
2 NT	limit bid on a flat hand with five hearts
3♣/3♢	second suit (forcing for one round)
3♡	limit bid on a 6-carder
3 NT	offering partner a choice of games

The 2♡ transfer

Similar, a 2♡ response shows five spades and the opener will usually rebid 2♠:

West	East
1 NT	2♡
2♠	?

On the second round responder has the same sort of options available:

2 NT	limit bid on a flat hand with 5 spades
3♣/3♢/3♡	second suit (forcing for one round)
3♠	limit bid on a 6-carder
3 NT	offering a choice of games

The 2♠ response

A response of 2♠ shows either a limit raise to 2 NT or a game-forcing hand where responder is looking for a 4-4 fit somewhere. The opener rebids on these lines:

2 NT	minimum
3 any	not minimum, lowest 4-card suit

The responder may pass 2 NT if his 2♠ call was based on the limit bid type; otherwise all sequences are forcing to game.

The 2 NT transfer

The 2 NT response is a transfer to 3♣ and shows one of three types:

(a) Weak with clubs (you pass opener's 3♣)
(b) Weak with diamonds (over 3♣ you bid 3◇)
(c) Strong with both minors (over 3♣ you bid a short major or 3 NT

Three-level responses

All three-level responses are game-forcing on a suit of at least 5 cards.

There are two main advantages in playing transfer responses. The 1 NT opener often becomes declarer, protecting his tenaces from the opening lead; also, many more sequences become available to responder.

The opener should not be reluctant to rebid with a jump when he holds four cards in the suit partner is showing. Even with this moderate hand:

♠ K 10 4 3   ♡ K 5   ◇ A J 2   ♣ Q 9 8 6

you follow the sequence 1 NT–2♡–3♠. If partner is fairly weak and you go one down, you can be sure that you are saving something. The same argument applies even more strongly when your suit is hearts, because you should want to make it difficult for the opponents to contest in spades.

These are some of the many transfer sequences available:

West	East
♠ K 7 6	♠ Q 10 9 6 5
♡ K J 10 3	♡ 8 5 4
◇ A Q 5	◇ 9 2
♣ J 6 4	♣ K 10 3

West	East
1 NT	2 ♡
2 ♠	End

East transfers the contract to West, thereby protecting West's tenaces from the opening lead.

West	East
♠ A 2	♠ J 5 3
♡ K 10 4	♡ A J 9 7 2
◇ K 9 7 4	◇ Q 10 6
♣ Q J 10 5	♣ K 2

West	East
1 NT	2 ◇
2 ♡	2 NT
4 ♡	End

East shows five hearts and the values for a raise to 2 NT. Playing transfers enables you to give the picture of five hearts and the values for 2 NT at an economical level. West, with just enough to accept the try, jumps to 4♡. Take away his ♣ J and he would bid only 3♡.

West	East
♠ K 8 2	♠ A Q 9 7 5
♡ K 9 4	♡ 10 2
◇ 10 6 5	◇ K Q 7 2
♣ A Q 8 3	♣ 9 4

West	East
1 NT	2 ♡
2 ♠	3 ◇
3 ♠	End

East shows two suits and a hand of at least game-try strength (his 3◇ is forcing for one round). West's hand was only just worth an opening bid in the first place and his holding in diamonds is unattractive. He signs off in 3♠.

West	East
♠ A 9 6 4	♠ K 10 4
♡ K Q 3	♡ J 9 4
♢ 9 8 6	♢ A Q 4 2
♣ K 10 4	♣ Q 7 3

West	East
1 NT	2 ♠
2 NT	End

West first assumes that East has a limit raise to 2 NT. Since his own hand is minimum he rebids just 2 NT, which on this occasion is passed out. Had East continued with a call such as 3♣ over 2 NT, he would have shown a strong hand (including a 4-card club suit) that was looking for a 4-card fit somewhere. West would continue with 3♠.

West	East
♠ K 9 3	♠ Q 7 4
♡ A Q 10 2	♡ 9 8 3
♢ Q 5 3	♢ A J 9 8 7 6
♣ K 5 4	♣ 8

West	East
1 NT	2 NT
3 ♣	3 ♢
End	

2 NT was a transfer to 3♣ and East's subsequent 3♢ call indicates a weakish hand with long diamonds. West is not invited to proceed.

Responding to 2 NT

There are two styles of responding to 2 NT: natural, as played in rubber bridge; and transfer, usual in the tournament game.

This is the natural scheme:

3 ♣	Stayman, asking for 4-card majors
3 ◇/3 ♡/3 ♠	5-card suit, at least, forcing to game
Game bids	to play
4 NT	limit bid, inviting a slam

Stayman works well when you are 5–4 in the majors:

West	East
♠ K Q 8	♠ A J 9 8 2
♡ A J 7	♡ 10 8 3 2
◇ K Q 10 4	◇ J 5
♣ A J 3	♣ 7 6

West	East
2 NT	3 ♣
3 ◇	3 ♠
4 ♠	End

East starts with Stayman. The opener denies a 4-card major but East continues with 3♠, showing a 5-card holding. West, with 3-card support, raises to the spade game. Note that 3 NT would not have been safe on a club lead.

West	East
♠ A J 5	♠ K 10 6 3
♡ A Q 10 3	♡ 7 5
◇ K 3	◇ A Q 9 7 2
♣ A Q 8 7	♣ J 2

West	East
2 NT	3 ◇
3 ♡	3 ♠
3 NT	End

East can visualize a slam if partner has a fit in one of his suits. He starts by bidding the 5-card diamonds. West shows four hearts and East four spades. If West had a diamond fit he would continue with 4◇. As it is, there is no fit and the pair come safely to a halt in 3 NT.

2-star convention: transfers opposite 2 NT

Again, more accuracy can be achieved by using transfer responses. This is the complete scheme:

3 ♣	Stayman, 4 cards in at least one major
3 ◇	at least 5 hearts
3 ♡	at least 5 spades
3 ♠	at least 5–4 in the minors
3 NT/4 ♡/4 ♠	to play
4 ♣/4 ◇	natural and forcing

These are common transfer sequences:

West	*East*
♠ A J 7 3	♠ 5 4
♡ K J 8	♡ A Q 7 6 2
◇ K Q	◇ J 9 4 2
♣ A K 7 3	♣ 6 2

West	*East*
2 NT	3 ◇
3 ♡	3 NT
4 ♡	End

East raises to 3 NT, showing five hearts on the way. West chooses to play in hearts. Had East been a little stronger, with ◇ A instead of ◇ J, he could have bid 4◇ at his second turn. The partnership would then advance to 6♡.

West	East
♠ A K J 5	♠ 4
♡ K Q J 3	♡ 10 2
♢ Q 8 2	♢ A J 9 4 3
♣ A 4	♣ K J 7 5 2

West	East
2 NT	3 ♠
3 NT	End

East shows interest in a minor-suit contract but West has his values packed in the majors and suggests that 3 NT will be the best spot. On his present hand East does not have enough to continue. Make his ♢ J the ♢ K and he would press on with 4♣.

2-star convention: Baron 3 ♣ response

In this alternative scheme to Stayman 3♣ asks for any 4-card suit, including diamonds. Both players show their 4-card suits until 3 NT is reached.

West	East
♠ K Q 2	♠ A 9 5 4
♡ A J 7 6	♡ 4 3
♢ K Q 8 5	♢ A J 6 4
♣ A Q	♣ K 9 2

West	East
2 NT	3 ♣
3 ♢	3 ♠
3 NT	4 ♢
4 ♡	6 ♢
End	

West's 3◇ response shows a diamond suit. East still bids his spades, in case there is a fit there. When West denies one, East shows the diamond fit. West cue-bids the ace of hearts and the pair arrive in the best slam. The main advantage of the Baron convention is that it becomes easier to reach minor-suit slams.

5

Responding to One of a Suit

When partner opens one of a suit there are many avenues open to you as responder. You may:

- (i) pass, which is usually right when you have less than 6 points;
- (ii) respond 1 NT, with around 6–9 points and no suit worth bidding at the one level;
- (iii) respond 2 NT with about 10–12 points and a flat hand;
- (iv) raise partner's suit to some level;
- (v) bid one of a new suit, usually 6 points or more;
- (vi) bid two of a new suit, usually 9 points or more;
- (vii) make various other higher bids.

With so many options it is not always easy to choose the right one. We will start by looking at some weak responding hands.

When you have a weak hand

Suppose it is love-all and partner opens 1♢ in first position. What response, if any, would you make on these uninspiring hands?

(1) ♠ A 10 9 7 6 2 ♡ 8 2 ♢ 6 4 ♣ 10 5 3

Bid 1♠. You don't hold the magic 6 points but a good spade suit is always worth a mention; you make it harder for the next player to introduce hearts. Swap the majors and there would be less reason for a 1♡ response.

(2) ♠ 9 7 4 ♥ Q J 5 3 ♦ 10 7 2 ♣ K 6 4

Here you respond 1♥. It would not be a mistake to pass, but once in a while partner will hold enough to make game. Apart from that, if you pass you will make it easy for the opponents to contest.

(3) ♠ J 7 6 2 ♥ J 9 3 ♦ 7 4 ♣ A J 8 4

1 NT is much better than 1♠ on such a poor suit.

On minimum hands with 4-card trump support for the minor which partner has opened, you may have to choose between raising partner and bidding a suit at the one-level:

(4) ♠ K Q 10 4 ♥ Q 5 ♦ J 10 6 2 ♣ 9 7 5

Bid 1♠ over 1♦. Although you have a diamond fit you are happy to show a good major suit.

(5) ♠ 10 8 7 ♥ Q 6 5 2 ♦ K 10 8 2 ♣ Q 9

Here it is not worth showing the spindly hearts; raise directly to 2♦.

Which suit to bid?

When you have a choice of suits in which to respond, these are the general guidelines:

  (i) With two 4-card suits normally bid the 'cheaper' one (make the bid that consumes least space).
 (ii) With one 5-card suit and one 4-card suit generally bid the longer suit first (unless that would necessitate a two-level response and you are too weak).
(iii) With two 5-card suits bid the higher suit first.

Bearing these guidelines in mind, how would you respond to 1 ♦ on these hands:

(6)   ♠ K 10 9 4   ♡ Q J 8 3   ◇ 10 6   ♣ K 3 2

Respond 1♡, bidding the cheaper of your two suits. Partner will have the chance to introduce spades.

(7)   ♠ A J 5 4   ♡ Q 10 4   ◇ 7 2   ♣ A K 8 3

Here it is usual to respond 1♠. A 2♣ response would not be a mistake, though; you are strong enough to continue with 2♠ and, if necessary, 3 NT.

(8)   ♠ 10 5   ♡ K Q 10 4   ◇ 6 3   ♣ A Q J 8 6

Bid 2♣, showing the longer suit first. Over a 2◇ rebid you will continue with 2♡, showing your suits in the natural order. Had your first response been 1♡ you would have had no sound call over a 2◇ rebid.

(9)   ♠ 8 4   ♡ K J 9 4   ◇ 10 4   ♣ K 9 7 6 3

Here you have to bid 1♡. You don't have the strength necessary to bid at the two-level. (You intend to pass a rebid of 2◇, of course.)

(10)   ♠ A J 8 5 2   ♡ K Q 10 9 3   ◇ K 2   ♣ 5

With two 5-card suits you respond in the higher, so here you bid 1♠ over 1◇. If partner rebids 1 NT or 2◇ you will jump to 3♡, showing a strong hand and a second suit. This sequence will promise at least five cards in spades, since with 4–4 in the majors you would have responded 1♡.

The 2 NT response

In traditional Acol the 2 NT response shows around 11 points and a balanced hand. Suppose you hold:

♠ J 8 4   ♡ A Q 5   ◇ J 10 5 4   ♣ K 9 4

If partner opens 1♣ there is little point in responding 1◇. Make a limit bid of 2NT directly, giving less information to the opponents. You can make the same response to 1◇. If instead partner opens 1♠, there's not much wrong with a 2NT response, but partner is likely to have five spades and the hand may play better in his suit. Take things slowly with a 2◇ response, hoping to show your 3-card support on the next round. You would make the same response to 1♡.

2-star convention: Baron 2NT response

Tournament players have mostly abandoned the 2NT response that shows about 11 points. Instead they use the Baron 2NT response, indicating a flat hand with at least 16 points. Such hands are notoriously difficult to bid in Acol.

Here is an example of the bid in use:

West	East
♠ A J 5 4 2	♠ 8 4
♡ K Q 7 4	♡ A J 8 2
◇ 10 2	◇ K Q 5
♣ Q 4	♣ A K 9 2

West	East
1 ♠	2NT[1]
3 ♡	4 ♡
End	

[1] Baron 2NT

East uses the Baron 2NT to show a flat hand with slam potential. He can then bid just 4♡ on the second round, leaving it to partner to make any further running. If West had, for example, the ace of diamonds instead of the 10, he would carry the bidding to 6♡. You can see that it would be difficult for East to express his hand after a start of 1♠–2♣–2♡.

A further advantage of the Baron 2 NT is that a jump in a suit (a sequence such as 1♠–3♣–3♠–3 NT) emphasizes the quality of the suit, clubs in this instance. With a 2–3–4–4-type, responder would have tried 2 NT instead.

Does playing this convention lead to problems when you hold a flat 11-count as responder? Not really. You mark time with a bid in a 4-card side suit (sometimes a lower valued three-card suit), intending to make a limit bid of 2 NT on the next round.

Other responses to one of a suit

The various responses when you have a good fit for partner's first suit will be discussed in the next chapter. Jump-shift responses (such as 1♡–2♠) will be covered in chapter 10.

6

Raising Partner's Suit Opening

When partner opens in a major

Suppose partner opens 1♡ or 1♠ and you have a hand with fair trump support. These are the options open to you, listed in ascending order of power:

   (i) single raise;
  (ii) double raise;
 (iii) game raise;
  (iv) delayed game raise (a sequence such as
         1♠–2◇–2♡–4♠);
   (v) stronger sequences, such as the Swiss convention or a
         jump shift.

We will consider them in turn.

The single raise

Raises, in general, are not based on points, and we do not recommend methods that seek to combine high-card points and distributional points. It is essential to acquire a natural sense of values.

A single raise will contain about 6–8 points more often than not, but distributional values, such as a singleton with four-card trump support, should be taken fully into account. Suppose partner has opened 1♠ and you hold:

(1) ♠ K 10 8 4 ♡ 9 7 2 ◇ Q J 4 3 ♣ 10 5

This is a typical raise to 2♠.

(2) ♠ K 10 7 3 ♡ 10 9 5 ◇ 5 ♣ 9 7 6 4 2

Again you raise to 2♠, if only for tactical reasons.

(3) ♠ Q 9 2 ♡ 8 4 ◇ A Q 5 2 ♣ J 10 7 4

Raise to 2♠ once more. Your partner is quite likely to hold five spades and the hand will play well in spades even if he holds only four.

The double raise

A double raise is strongly invitational but non-forcing. It will usually reflect 9–11 points, but again distributional values are equally important. How would you evaluate these hands when your partner opens 1♡?

(4) ♠ 9 7 2 ♡ A K 7 2 ◇ 10 8 ♣ K 10 5 2

You raise to 3♡. Partner will then pass only if he is minimum in terms of both points and distribution.

(5) ♠ K 3 ♡ A 10 5 4 2 ◇ 10 8 5 2 ♣ 7 6

Again you're worth a raise to three. Both your doubletons are 'working' because, with five trumps in the dummy, partner will have no problem in taking his ruffs.

The direct game raise

This type of responding hand falls into two categories:

  (i) flat hands with 4-card support and around 12–13 points,
  (ii) distributional hands with good trump support, where the raise is partly pre-emptive.

Partner opens 1♠ and you hold one of these hands:

(6) ♠ Q J 5 4 ♡ 8 4 ◇ K Q 2 ♣ K Q 6 3

Raise to 4♠. You want to be in game, but with so few controls the chance of a slam is poor.

(7) ♠ K 10 8 7 2 ♡ 7 ◇ K J 9 4 2 ♣ 9 5

Again you bid 4♠. This is the other type of game raise. You hope to make the game, naturally, but you are also keen to deter the opponents, who may have a big fit somewhere themselves.

Delayed game raise

Since a direct raise to game is a limited call, expressing no enthusiasm for any slam ventures, you must choose a different route when your hand is a bit stronger. One possibility is to bid a new suit first, then raise partner to game. Suppose partner has opened 1♡ and you are staring at this promising collection:

(8) ♠ 2 ♡ K Q 8 5 ◇ J 10 4 ♣ A K J 10 3

This may yield a slam facing as little as ♠ A x ♡ A J x x x ◇ K x x x ♣ Q x. Since you have a good side suit you can start by responding 2♣. If partner rebids 2◇ you bid 4♡ at your second turn. Since you obviously had heart support all along, but chose to show a side suit first, partner will realize that you were too strong for a direct raise to game. This type of sequence is known as a delayed game raise.

There is an important distinction between these two sequences:

(i)	*West*	*East*		(ii)	*West*	*East*
	1 ♡	2 ♣			1 ♡	2 ♣
	2 ◇	4 ♡			2 ♡	4 ♡

The auction on the left is a true delayed game raise. In the other auction West rebid his hearts and East does not guarantee

33

'delayed game raise' values. He may not even hold four hearts, since West has rebid his heart suit. (When responder does still wish to deliver a 'delayed game raise' message he may jump to four in the other minor, here 4♢.)

1-star convention: Swiss responses

What do you do when you are too strong for a direct raise to game but have no good side suit for a delayed game raise? The answer is that you assign some conventional meaning to the responses at the four-level. This is one simple scheme, known as the Swiss Convention. After an opening of 1♡ or 1♠ you may make these responses:

4♣   A game raise containing good controls. There is room for the opener to express interest below game level.

4♢   A game raise with good trumps, not shapely.

This scheme is easy to remember and performs a useful function. Tournament players may prefer to use something a little more sophisticated, such as . . .

2-star convention: Four-barrelled Swiss

This version of Swiss covers both flat hands and those that contain a side suit singleton. The responder to 1♡ may make one of these calls:

3♠   Showing a sound game raise including a singleton; the opener may then ask for the singleton by bidding 3 NT and the responder bids:

   4♣   with a singleton club,
   4♢   with a singleton diamond,
   4♡   with a singleton spade.

3 NT Showing a sound game raise, no singleton, and 1 of the
5 'aces' (♡ K counting as an ace).

4♣ The same, with 2 of the 5 'aces'.

4♢ The same, with 3 of the 5 'aces'.

Opposite 1♠ the responses are similar. 3 NT shows a sound
raise with a singleton (and 4♣ then enquires which singleton),
4♣/4♢/4♡ show a flat raise with 1/2/3 of the 5 'aces'.

Let's see this convention in action.

West	East
♠ A K J 8 4 3	♠ Q 9 6 2
♡ K 2	♡ A J 6 5
♢ J 8 3	♢ 5
♣ K 10	♣ A Q 7 4

West	East
1 ♠	3 NT
4 ♣	4 ♢
4 NT	5 ♡
6 ♠	End

East shows a sound game raise with a singleton. West asks for
the singleton and East says it's in diamonds. This is good news;
it means that West can ruff two of his diamond losers. He
launches into Blackwood and bids the slam.

If you swap East's minors he would have responded 4♠ at his
second turn, showing a club singleton. West, knowing that the
fit was not a good one, would then pass.

Jump shift with a fit

When you have a trump fit, a good side suit, and are too strong
for a delayed game raise, you begin with a jump in the side suit.
We will look in detail at the jump shift in Chapter 10. Meanwhile, here is one sequence where the responder has a trump fit.

West	East
♠ A J 8 4	♠ 10 3
♡ K J 9 7 5 2	♡ A Q 6 4
♢ Q 8	♢ J 4
♣ 7	♣ A K Q 10 5

West	East
1 ♡	3 ♣
3 ♡	4 ♡
End	

East, having issued a strong slam invitation, bids a modest 4♡ on the next round. West, with an uninspiring hand and only one ace, lets the bidding die. With an extra control, such as ♢ K instead of ♢ Q, he would have made a further move towards a slam.

When partner opens one of a minor

The situation is not quite the same when partner has opened with one of a minor. These are the main differences:

(i) you should not raise with only 3-card trump support,
(ii) if the opening might be a 'prepared club', you need 5 clubs to raise,
(iii) a double raise (such as 1♢–3♢) may contain more in points than a similar raise in a major. You may wish to keep below 3 NT.

Suppose partner has opened 1♢ and you hold any of these hands:

(9)   ♠ Q 3   ♡ 10 8 7 6   ♢ K 5 4   ♣ K 10 7 2

Don't raise the diamonds on just 3-card support; respond 1 NT. There are those who consider it a duty to respond in the 4-card major; we would regard that as fatuous here.

(10) ♠ A 10 7 ♡ 9 8 ◇ A Q J 7 2 ♣ 7 6 4

Here you raise to just 3◇, keeping below the most likely game –
3 NT. If you were supporting a major-suit opening with such
values, you would raise to the four-level.

(11) ♠ A 8 3 ♡ J 3 ◇ A K 10 5 2 ♣ Q 10 3

Give yourself a few more points and you arrive at a tricky
bidding problem. A raise of 1◇ to 3◇ is non-forcing, so what
can you bid on this healthy 14-count? Unless you play a convention such as minor-suit Swiss (see below), you have to invent a
bid. Some players would call 2♣, or even 1♠; others would
respond 3 NT, trusting to fortune in the heart suit.

(12) ♠ 4 ♡ A 3 ◇ K Q 10 9 6 2 ♣ J 8 7 3

On this hand you would make the rare call of raising 1◇ to 4◇.
The bid shows a limited, very distributional hand, where 3 NT
is unlikely to be the right spot.

1-star convention: minor-suit Swiss

As we saw above, a small bidding problem arises when you have
game values and a fit for partner's minor suit but no suit of your
own to call. One solution is to assign artificial meanings to
double-jump responses such as 1♣–3♡. Traditionally such a
response is pre-emptive, indicating a weak hand with a long
major. In a version of minor-suit Swiss suggested by Hugh
Kelsey, such calls indicate strong support for partner's minor
(around 12–15 high-card points) and a good stop in the suit
shown.

Here is an example of the convention at work:

West	East
♠ K J 5	♠ A Q 4
♡ 9 3	♡ 8 4 2
◇ A Q 9 7 2	◇ K J 10 5 4
♣ A J 6	♣ K 3

West	East
1 ◇	3 ♠
5 ◇	End

The danger in hearts is made obvious to West. He has the values to attempt a minor-suit game, though, so he jumps to 5◇. A call of 4◇ would have been non-forcing.

The Opener's Rebid

We cover this area in the following order:

  (i) the opener rebids his own suit;
 (ii) he raises his partner's suit;
(iii) he rebids in notrumps;
 (iv) he rebids in a new suit.

The calls in the first three categories are all limit bids. Only when the opener rebids in a new suit (in a sequence such as 1♠–2♣–2◇) is the strength of his hand still relatively unknown.

The opener rebids his suit

When the opener rebids his suit at the minimum level he suggests a hand in the 11–14 range.

    (1) ♠ K 4   ♡ A Q 10 5 3 2   ◇ Q 6 4   ♣ Q 9

Absolutely straightforward. You open 1♡ and rebid 2♡ over 1 NT or any change of suit.

    (2) ♠ A Q 8 5 2   ♡ A 6   ◇ K 10 5 4   ♣ 10 3

You open 1♠. When partner responds 2♣ you will find some players who rebid 2♠ ('to let you know I was weak, partner'). Such calls indicate that the player is just as weak as his hand! You should rebid 2◇, of course, which promises no more strength and describes your hand better.

If, instead, partner responds 2♡, then you must rebid 2♠ because a rebid of 3◇ would carry the bidding too high and indicate a much stronger hand.

(3)   ♠ K 10 5 4   ♡ A K J 9 3   ◇ Q 4   ♣ 10 5

Suppose you can open 1♡ and partner gives you two of a minor. You must rebid 2♡ because a call of 2♠ would again carry the bidding too high (past the safety barrier of two of your long suit). In general, bids that force the auction to a higher level must be backed by a hand containing the extra strength to play at that level.

When the opener makes a jump rebid in his own suit he indicates around 15–17 points, perhaps slightly less if he has a long suit. The call is forcing if partner's response was at the two-level.

(4)   ♠ A Q 4   ♡ 6   ◇ A K J 9 6 3   ♣ J 6 3

Here you open 1◇ and, opposite a 1 NT or minimum suit response, rebid 3◇. Since you can make 3 NT opposite the right 9-count, a rebid of just 2◇ would be inadequate.

(5)   ♠ A 3   ♡ K Q J 9 6 5   ◇ J 2   ♣ A J 5

You open 1♡, intending to rebid 3♡. This will be non-forcing opposite a 1♠ or 1 NT response, forcing opposite a two-level response.

With a long and strong suit you may rebid at the four-level.

(6)   ♠ K 4   ♡ A K J 10 7 6 2   ◇ 3   ♣ K 10 6

After 1♡–1♠ you rebid 4♡. If, instead, partner responds at the two-level, save space by rebidding 3♡ (forcing).

The opener raises partner's suit

Simple stuff here – the higher you raise partner, the stronger you are. Suppose you open 1◇ on this hand:

(7) ♠ K 10 5 4 ♥ 8 3 ♦ A Q 9 5 2 ♣ K 2

If partner responds 1♠ you give him 2♠, indicating a minimum hand. Make your hearts A x or K x and you would raise to 3♠ instead. With AQ or AK in hearts you would be worth 4♠.

With a minimum hand containing 3-card support a direct raise is often the best answer:

(8) ♠ 10 7 2 ♥ 6 ♦ A Q 7 5 3 ♣ K Q 9 2

You open 1♦ and partner says 1♠. Give him 2♠.

Suppose you are stronger:

(9) ♠ J 9 3 ♥ 4 ♦ A Q 7 6 2 ♣ A Q J 4

Now it is better to rebid 2♣, a less limited call. You intend to support the spades at your next turn.

The opener rebids in notrumps

We covered the rebid of 1 NT in Chapter 1. When playing a weak notrump, you will remember, the 1 NT rebid is 15–16; playing a strong notrump, 12–14.

Higher rebids in notrumps have fixed meanings, whatever opening 1 NT you play:

1♦–1♥–2 NT	17–18 points
1♥–2♣–2 NT	15–16 points
1♥–1♠–3 NT	19–20 points
1♠–2♣–3 NT	17–19 points

This is the traditional scheme but it has to be said that the 3 NT rebid is space-consuming and can cause problems. Look at this hand:

West	East
♠ A 9 4	♠ J 3
♡ K Q 10 9 3	♡ J 8 2
◇ A K J	◇ 10 7 3
♣ 7 4	♣ A Q J 8 2

West	East
1 ♡	2 ♣
3 NT	End

Four hearts would be a safer game but East has no way of knowing this. The auction is too high for any further investigation. There is a solution available . . .

1-star convention: 2 NT rebid game-forcing

When the bidding starts 1♠–2♣–2 NT, the opener has shown at least 15 points and the responder at least 9. It is therefore very unusual for the bidding to die below game. There are good grounds for making such 2 NT rebids forcing to game. This allows more space for investigation:

West	East
♠ A 9 4	♠ J 3
♡ K Q 10 9 3	♡ J 8 2
◇ A K J	◇ 10 7 3
♣ 7 4	♣ A Q J 8 2

West	East
1 ♡	2 ♣
2 NT	3 ♡
4 ◇	4 ♡
End	

These are the same hands we looked at a moment ago. When you play the 2 NT rebid as forcing, responder has the space to investigate 5–3 fits. West even had the opportunity to cue-bid 4◇, showing his suitability for a slam.

Here is a similar hand:

West	East
♠ A J 8 5	♠ K Q 7 3
♡ K Q 8 7	♡ J 2
♢ A 3 2	♢ 8 5
♣ K 4	♣ A J 8 7 2

West	East
1 ♡	2 ♣
2 NT	3 ♠
4 ♠	End

Had West not been playing '2 NT forcing to game', he might have rebid 3 NT, causing the spade fit to be missed.

The opener bids a new suit

The opener's final option is to make a further exploratory move in a new suit. Suppose the bidding has started like this:

West	East
1 ♢	1 ♠
?	

West may make three different types of suit rebid:

2♣   a rebid below two of the opener's suit covers a wide range of hands (about 12–17 points).

2♡   a rebid above two of the opener's suit (a reverse) shows at least 16 points or particularly strong distribution.

3♣   a jump rebid in a new suit is forcing to game.

Here are some typical hands:

(10)   ♠ 4 3   ♡ A 8   ♢ K Q 8 7 3   ♣ K 10 5 2

This is a dead minimum hand. After 1♢–1♠ you would rebid 2♣. (If playing a strong notrump you might prefer 1 NT.)

(11) ♠ 2 ♡ A J ◇ A Q J 6 4 ♣ K Q 9 7 5

Here you are much stronger, with 17 points. You can hardly rebid 3♣, though, which would be forcing to game. You again have to rebid 2♣. Make the clubs A Q 10 x x and the scales would topple; you would rebid 3♣.

(12) ♠ Q 4 ♡ K Q 6 5 ◇ A J 9 8 2 ♣ J 3

After 1◇–2♣ you must rebid 2◇, not 2♡.

(13) ♠ A 3 ♡ A Q 10 5 ◇ K Q J 3 2 ♣ J 6

Here you do have the necessary strength for a reverse. After 1◇–1♠ you rebid 2♡. The word 'always' is rarely used in bridge; when you reverse, though, your first suit is always assumed to be longer than your second.

When partner has responded at the two-level you may reverse on slightly fewer points. Suppose the bidding has started 1♡–2♣ and you hold this hand:

(14) ♠ A Q J 2 ♡ K Q 10 7 3 ◇ A 8 ♣ 10 2

Partner has suggested at least 9 points, so you can rebid 2♠ – a reverse. Following a two-level response, such a rebid is best played as forcing to game.

Here is a different sequence that, while not exactly a 'reverse', shows reversing values. The bidding has started 1♠–2◇ and you hold:

(15) ♠ K Q J 7 6 ♡ A 3 ◇ J 5 ♣ A Q 4 2

You rebid 3♣. Again this is beyond the safety net of two of your first suit, so the call shows extra strength. When you make such a non-jump rebid at the three-level it is known as a 'high reverse'. The call is forcing to game.

1-star convention: new suit forcing over two-level response

When partner has responded at the two-level, many tournament players treat a change of suit by opener (a sequence such as 1♠–2♣–2♦) as forcing. This gives the partnership more space to investigate, a telling advantage on hands of this type:

    (16)   ♠ A Q J 7 6 ♡ A K J 3 ♦ 7 ♣ Q 10 2

After 1♠–2♣ you rebid a simple 2♡ (forcing). Your best spot may be in spades, hearts, clubs or notrumps. If your system requires you to bid 3♡ to preserve a force, this is a considerable handicap.

    When a simple change of suit is forcing, a jump shift will signify support for partner's suit.

    (17)   ♠ K Q 10 7 2 ♡ 4 ♦ A Q 8 ♣ A J 9 2

After 1♠– 2♣ you rebid 3♦. With a single call you show strong support for clubs, a useful fragment in diamonds, and probably a shortage in hearts.

8

The Responder's Second Call

Unless the first three bids are in different suits (an auction such as 1♠–2♣–2♦), one or both players will have made a limit bid by the time the responder considers his second call. So, on many auctions the responder will merely have to add his values to those shown by the opener. He may then decide to sign off, make a game try, or bid a game somewhere. If none of these is appropriate, or a slam is possible, the responder may make some further exploratory move.

We will cover the subject in the following order:

  (i) the opener has rebid his suit;
 (ii) the opener has raised partner's suit;
(iii) the opener has rebid in notrumps;
(iv) the opener has bid a new suit.

When the opener has rebid his suit

Suppose the opener has indicated a limited hand with a sequence of 1♦–1♠–2♦. How would you continue on these responding hands?

  (1)   ♠ Q 10 8 6 5 2 ♡ K 9 7 3 ♦ J ♣ 9 2

Don't bid 2♠ or 2♡, giving partner a chance to take the bidding higher. Just pass 2♦.

(2) ♠ A Q 10 5 4 ♡ K J 8 2 ◇ 8 3 ♣ 10 7

Here you are stronger and game is not impossible. Advance to 2♡. This is a non-forcing call but partner is invited to proceed unless his hand is markedly unsuitable.

(3) ♠ K Q 10 4 ♡ J 9 3 ◇ 7 6 ♣ A J 9 4

You have the strength to invite game, so call 2 NT. No matter that you have an insecure heart holding; partner's opening bid will surely include cover there.

(4) ♠ A Q 10 8 7 6 ♡ A 2 ◇ 10 9 3 ♣ J 3

Again you want to invite game. Jump to 3♠, non-forcing but showing good values.

When the opener makes a jump rebid in a minor the target will often be 3 NT. As responder you may introduce a suit where you hold high cards but not necessarily length. Suppose, after a start of 1♣–1♠–3♣, you have to find a bid on this hand:

(5) ♠ K J 9 5 4 ♡ 8 6 5 ◇ A J 4 ♣ Q 3

Your best call is 3◇. If partner has heart values he will bid 3 NT now. If instead he marks time with 3♡, expressing doubt on the matter, you will bid your spades again, leaving all avenues open.

(6) ♠ K Q 10 9 7 ♡ Q 4 ◇ J 9 7 2 ♣ Q 5

This time, after 1♣–1♠–3♣, you continue with 3♠. This is forcing since with a weak hand you can simply pass 3♣.

After a response at the two-level a jump rebid by the opener (1♡–2♣–3♡) is forcing. After such a start to the auction how would you continue on this:

(7) ♠ A 8 3 ♡ 10 ◇ 9 7 3 2 ♣ A Q 9 7 6

Don't bid 3 NT now and find that either the spades or the diamonds are fatally weak. The right call is 4♡; your partner has indicated a powerful suit and your two aces will be a welcome sight in the dummy.

47

When the opener has raised your suit

You are standing on firm ground when the opener raises your suit. He has indicated his own strength and it just remains for you to add your own and announce the result. After a start of 1◇–1♠–2♠ you hold:

(8)   ♠ Q 10 8 7 5   ♡ A 7 6   ◇ 5 2   ♣ Q 9 6

No problem here. Partner has shown a limited hand and you have nothing special, so you pass. Make ♣Q into ♣A and you would invite game with a raise to 3♠. Make the clubs A–Q–x and you would raise to 4♠. You may apply the well-known test: opening values opposite opening values, plus a reasonable fit, add up to game.

(9)   ♠ K J 7 6   ♡ A 9 8   ◇ 6 2   ♣ K 10 9 3

Here again, after 1◇–1♠–2♠, you would like to invite game. Bid 2 NT. Such a game try will warn partner that you may have only four spades. Remember that he may have given you a single raise on only three trumps.

(10)   ♠ A J 8 7   ♡ J 9 2   ◇ A 3   ♣ K J 8 7

Here you will bid 3♣ at your second turn. Partner will read this as a game try at first and may sign off in 3♠ if he has a minimum. You will then continue with 3 NT, offering him a choice of games. He will know that you have only four spades and better clubs than hearts.

    When your hand is so strong that a slam may be possible you must make a cue bid. We will describe these fully in Chapter 14. In the meantime here is just one example:

(11)   ♠ A Q 10 8 7   ♡ 10 9 2   ◇ Q 3   ♣ A Q 7

After 1◇–1♠–3♠ you bid 4♣. This is a cue bid, suggesting a slam. It shows the ace or king of clubs, or possibly a singleton, and invites partner to respond in kind if he sees slam prospects. More of this later!

When the opener has rebid in notrumps

Here again the responder will have a good picture of the opener's strength and will often be able to announce the final contract immediately. We will look at various responding hands in ascending order of strength.

(12) ♠ 8 7 ♡ K Q 6 2 ◇ 10 9 4 2 ♣ A 5

The auction has started 1♣–1♡–1 NT. If this rebid shows 12–14 (because you are playing a 15–17 1 NT opening), you will obviously pass. If you are playing the weak notrump and the rebid therefore shows 15–16 points, you are worth 2 NT.

(13) ♠ K J 7 5 3 2 ♡ J 5 ◇ K 9 ♣ 10 4 2

After 1♡–1♠–1 NT you sign off in 2♠ if the 1 NT rebid is weak, invite game with 3♠ if it's strong.

Many misunderstandings arise about the forcing nature of calls when the responder returns to the opener's suit at the three level:

  (i)   1◇–1♠–1 NT–3◇
  (ii) 1♡–1♠–1 NT–3♡
  (iii) 1♡–2◇–2 NT–3♡

Simplest is to play that such calls are non-forcing in a minor, as in (i), and forcing in a major.

(14) ♠ 8 2 ♡ K J 3 ◇ A K 10 7 2 ♣ 9 6 2

After 1♡–2◇–2 NT you want to call 3♡ (forcing), in case partner has a 5-card heart suit.

When partner makes a jump rebid of 2 NT you have only two weak actions open to you: either pass or repeat your own suit at the minimum level. Other actions, such as a return to the opener's suit, are forcing.

(15) ♠ K J 9 8 5 2   ♡ J 4   ♢ 7 6   ♣ 10 8 2

After 1♢–1♠–2NT you throw a wet blanket on proceedings
with a 3♠ call. This is non-forcing but partner may still advance
when he has some spade support and his values are in aces and
kings rather than minor honours.

(16) ♠ K Q 10 6 3   ♡ A 7 2   ♢ K 7   ♣ Q 10 4

This time, again after 1♢–1♠– 2NT, there's the whiff of a slam
in the air, particularly if partner has 3-card spade support. You
can't bid 3♠, which would be non-forcing, so you must invent
a call . . . 3♣ on this occasion. Partner will take such a bid with a
pinch of salt, realizing that you may be angling for spade support. If he inopportunely raises the clubs the odds are that 6 NT
will be playable.

2-star convention: Crowhurst

In standard bidding the 1 NT rebid shows a hand of the opposite
strength to that of a 1 NT opening. Some players prefer to have
the freedom to rebid 1 NT on any hand in the 12–16 point range.
They then use a 2♣ bid by responder for further investigation.

Playing this scheme, invented by Eric Crowhurst, the bidding
may start:

1♡–1♠–1 NT–2♣–?

The opener then rebids:

   (i) 2 NT on any 15–16 point hand (forcing to game);
  (ii) 2♡ if he has 5 hearts (12–14);
 (iii) 2♠ if he has 3 spades (12–14);
  (iv) 2♢ otherwise.

Here is an example of the convention in action:

West	East
♠ K 10 3	♠ Q J 9 5 4
♡ K 4	♡ J 3
♢ A Q 5 4	♢ K 8 3
♣ K J 9 3	♣ A 7 2

West	East
1 ♢	1 ♠
1 NT	2 ♣
2 NT	3 ♠
4 ♠	End

West is playing a weak notrump, so he opens 1 ♢. His 1 NT is wide-range (12–16) and East enquires with a Crowhurst 2 ♣ call. The 2 NT rebid shows 15–16 and is forcing to game; when East repeats his spades West is happy to raise.

Playing a standard system, the bidding would start 1 ♢–1 ♠– 1 NT and East would have no sure way to investigate a 5–3 spade fit.

An obvious disadvantage of the wide-range 1 NT rebid is that responder with 9 or 10 points may have to advance beyond 1 NT, just in case the magic 25 points are present. This will leave him in no-man's land when the opener has a minimum 12 points.

If you don't like the idea of a wide-range 1 NT rebid, it is still possible to play 2 ♣ as an artificial enquiry to investigate major-suit fits.

The opener has rebid in a new suit

We will look first at the situation where the opener has made a simple rebid, compatible with a minimum holding. Look at this start to the auction, for example:

	West	East
	1 ♡	1 ♠
	2 ◇	?

East may choose from these actions:

  (i) Weak calls: Pass, 2♡, 2♠.
 (ii) Game-try calls: 2 NT, 3◇, 3♡, 3♠.
(iii) Game calls: 3 NT, 4♡, 4♠.
(iv) Fourth-suit: 3♣.

East's choice of call will be based on the initial assumption that his partner is minimum for the 2◇ rebid. Here are some possible hands for the responder:

  (17)   ♠ A J 8 7   ♡ 6 5 2   ◇ J 2   ♣ Q 8 7 3

Here you would bid 2♡, a simple return to opener's first suit. Such a call promises no extra strength whatsoever. You would make the same call on a hand such as this:

  (18)   ♠ K 10 9 3   ♡ 9 7   ◇ Q 4   ♣ Q 10 6 5 2

Partner's hearts are likely to be at least as long as his diamonds, so when you bid 2♡ over 2◇ you are merely saying 'I prefer to play there'. Partner has no reason to think you have support for his trump suit.

  (19)   ♠ A J 10 7 6 2   ♡ 5   ◇ K 4 3   ♣ J 9 8

Here you rebid 2♠. Again this is a limited call and partner will advance only if repetition of the spades improves the look of his hand.

It's time to look at some slightly stronger hands where you would like to invite game. On the next few hands, suppose the bidding has started:

	West	East
	1 ◇	1 ♡
	1 ♠	?

(20) ♠ K 10 8 6 ♡ A J 6 5 2 ◇ 8 3 ♣ J 2

No problem here. You have support for partner's second suit, so you make a limit raise to 3♠. Such a call is invitational but non-forcing. Had your ♣J been ♣K, you would have raised to 4♠.

(21) ♠ J 7 ♡ K Q 10 6 5 ◇ 8 2 ♣ A J 9 4

Again you have around 11 points, the values for a game try. You call 2 NT, showing a flattish hand with a secure stop in the unbid suit. Partner will generally pass if he has a weak hand. If instead he makes a call such as 3♡, this will be forcing and will show 3-card heart support.

(22) ♠ K 3 ♡ K Q J 9 6 5 ◇ Q 3 ♣ 10 6 2

Once more an invitational call is right. After 1◇–1♡–1♠ you bid 3♡, showing around 11 points and a good 6-card suit.

When you have 13 points or more, or a particularly long suit or good fit, you may be able to bid a game at your second turn:

(23) ♠ J 2 ♡ A Q J 9 6 3 2 ◇ 4 ♣ K 9 2

Here you bid 4♡ at your second turn, showing game values and a self-supporting suit.

Sometimes you will have a good hand but still not be sure of the best place to play. Suppose the auction has started 1♠–2♣–2◇ and you hold this collection:

(24) ♠ J 2 ♡ A 4 ◇ A J 2 ♣ K J 9 5 4 2

The best final contract might be 3 NT, 4♠, 5♣, 5◇, or various slams. You need more information before you can decide. Meanwhile, what bid can you make? A simple rebid of your suit, 3♣, would be non-forcing; so would limit bids such as 3◇ and 3♠.

The solution on such hands is to bid the fourth suit, here 2♡. Such a call indicates good values and asks partner to describe his hand further. It says nothing about your holding in the fourth suit itself; it's likely you don't hold much there, in fact, or perhaps you would have bid notrumps at this stage.

Fourth-suit bidding is so important that we have devoted a whole chapter to it (Chapter 9). Meanwhile, here is a complete auction that involves the hand above (24):

West	East
♠ A Q 10 5 4	♠ J 2
♡ J 3	♡ A 4
♢ K 10 5 4	♢ A J 2
♣ Q 3	♣ K J 9 5 4 2

West	East
1 ♠	2 ♣
2 ♢	2 ♡
3 ♣	3 ♢
3 ♠	4 ♠
End	

West shows his secondary support for the responder's main suit, then stresses his robust spades. You see the breathing space that was given to the auction by the fourth-suit call. There was time to investigate the various possible games.

The opener has reversed

When the opener has indicated extra values by rebidding in a suit higher than his first suit, the bidding proceeds in much the same way as we have just seen. The bidding has begun:

West	East
1 ♢	1 ♠
2 ♡	?

East may now pass, following his response at the one-level. Calls of 2♠ and 3♢ would be non-forcing; all other calls are forcing to game. In particular, it is best to play that 2NT is forcing; otherwise East has to waste space by jumping to 3NT, when this may well not be the best spot.

When the responder has bid at the two-level a reverse by opener is game-forcing. The responder should not therefore jump at his second turn unless he has a particular message to convey:

West	*East*
1♡	2♢
2♠	3NT
End	

East holds:

♠ Q 3
♡ 9 4
♢ A J 9 4 3
♣ K J 10 7

East takes the opportunity to show additional values that would otherwise not be easy to express later.

Fourth-suit Forcing

As we noted in the previous chapter, when the auction starts with three suit bids (1♠–2♣–2♢, for example), the responder will sometimes hold a hand worth game, or nearly so, where no natural bid is satisfactory. On such occasions he may use an artificial device – he may bid the *fourth suit*. Such a call asks partner to continue to describe his hand.

Suppose the bidding starts:

West	East
1 ♠	2 ♣
2 ♢	?

As East, you must find a second call on this hand:

(1)   ♠ 9 4 ♡ 10 8 7 ♢ A Q 5 ♣ A K J 7 6

You have the values for game, but which game? It could be 3 NT, 4♠, 5♣ or 5♢. You need further information about partner's hand. No remotely satisfactory natural bid is available, so you bid 2♡ – the fourth suit. This is hardly needed in a natural sense anyway; if you had values in hearts you would doubtless be calling notrumps at this stage.

After the same start (1♠–2♣–2♢) you might hold:

(2)   ♠ 7 ♡ A 6 3 ♢ Q 10 7 2 ♣ A Q 8 3 2

You have support for partner's diamonds but 3♢ would be a non-forcing limit bid; 4♢ is hardly attractive because this would carry the partnership beyond 3 NT. Again the solution is to show your strength with a fourth-suit bid of 2♡. If partner's next move is to bid 2♠ or 3♣, you will continue with 3◇, which will now be *forcing*. Bids which would have been limit bids when made directly become forcing when made via the fourth suit.

The same is true when responder wants to rebid his own suit.

(3)   ♠ A Q 9 7 6 3   ♡ A 4   ◇ 10 7   ♣ Q J 3

After 1◇–1♠ (by you)–2♣ you cannot rebid 3♠ because this would be non-forcing. Instead you show your strength with a 2♡ call, intending to bid 3♠ (now forcing) on the next round.

The hands we have seen so far were hands that would eventually arrive in game. Sometimes the fourth-suit bidder holds a bit less.

(4)   ♠ A Q 10 7 6   ♡ J 8 2   ◇ 9 4   ♣ A 9 3

After 1◇–1♠–2♣ no natural call is attractive. You bid 2♡, the fourth suit, requesting more information from partner.

The fourth suit should always indicate fair values, though. It is quite wrong to introduce such a bid on a hand of 8 or 9 points, merely because you cannot find a good call.

Responding to a fourth-suit call

The first thing to establish is which rebids by opener over the fourth suit are forcing. This scheme is both simplest and best:

After responder has bid the fourth suit, any rebid by the opener at the two level is non-forcing; any higher rebid is game-forcing.

Suppose that the auction starts like this:

West	East
1 ♡	1 ♠
2 ♣	2 ◇
?	

If West rebids 2♡, 2♠ or 2NT now, this will be non-forcing.

Any higher call will be forcing to game.

Bearing this in mind, let's look at some possible hands for West.

(5) ♠ 10 3 ♥ A Q 8 7 2 ♦ Q 6 ♣ K Q 10 2

With nothing much to spare for his opening, West must look for a non-forcing call at this stage. The diamond holding is insufficient for 2NT (remember that partner has guaranteed nothing in diamonds). Best is 2♠. Partner has no right to expect three spades for this call since with most 3–5–1–4 hands you would have rebid 2♠ on the previous round (or would be bidding 3♠ now).

(6) ♠ 7 ♥ A K 10 9 3 ♦ K 10 3 ♣ A J 8 2

Here you do have a secure diamond stop. 2NT would be non-forcing, though, so you must bid 3NT.

A raise of the artificial fourth-suit call traditionally shows a 4-card holding there and more than a minimum hand. This is a rare type of hand, though, and in the tournament world the bid is more often used to indicate general strength but no good bid to make.

(7) ♠ 6 ♥ A Q J 6 5 ♦ A 6 5 ♣ A Q 8 4

Once more the bidding starts 1♥–1♠–2♣–2♦. It is not attractive to bid 3NT on ace-to-three; the contract may play better from partner's side. Also, your hand has good slam potential if partner has a fit for one of your suits. Best is to bid 3♦, raising the fourth-suit bid. Partner will place you with this type of hand.

Fourth-suit bid by the opener

The opener, too, can make use of fourth-suit bids.

(8) ♠ 7 6 ♥ J 9 2 ♦ A 8 ♣ A K J 10 4 2

You open 1♣ and the bidding proceeds 1♣–1♠–2♣–3♢. Your heart stop is hardly adequate to risk a 3 NT call. The solution is make a fourth-suit call of 3♡. Partner will not bid 3 NT unless he himself has something helpful in hearts.

Completing the auction

Let's see some full auctions involving a fourth-suit call.

West	East
♠ K J 7	♠ A Q 7 3
♡ A Q 8 5 3	♡ J 6
♢ A J 7 6	♢ K 5
♣ 3	♣ A Q 10 4 2

West	East
1 ♡	2 ♣
2 ♢	2 ♠
3 NT	4 NT
Pass	

East, too strong to bid 3 NT over 2♢, resorts to the fourth suit. When his partner jumps to 3 NT East can see the glimmer of a slam. He makes an invitational raise to 4 NT (not Blackwood because no suit has been agreed). West has a singleton in his partner's main suit and his hand is lacking in middle cards (look how useful ♡10 would be, for example). He therefore declines the invitation.

59

West	East
♠ A Q 9 7 4	♠ 10 8 7
♡ K J 8 6	♡ A Q
◇ K 6	◇ 9 3 2
♣ 8 7	♣ A Q J 6 3

West	East
1 ♠	2 ♣
2 ♡	3 ◇
3 NT	4 ♠
Pass	

When East hears the 2♡ rebid he knows he would like to play in 4♠. If he bids 4♠ directly over 2♡, though, partner will take him for a 'delayed game raise' (see Chapter 6). To cancel that message, he bids the fourth suit first, then 4♠.

West	East
♠ A J 8 7 2	♠ K 3
♡ 2	♡ Q 10 4
◇ A J 9 4 3	◇ K Q 2
♣ K 6	♣ A Q 10 4 3

West	East
1 ♠	2 ♣
2 ◇	2 ♡
3 ◇	4 ◇
4 ♡	4 NT
5 ♡	6 ◇
Pass	

East had an adequate heart stop to venture 3 NT at his second call. However, he had no reason to think this was the best contract; 4♠ or 5◇ might be better; a slam was also possible. The fourth-suit call of 2♡ kept all options open. When the 5–3 diamond fit came to light and West cue-bid in hearts, East bid the slam via Blackwood. The special value of the convention here was that West, knowing his side was well afloat, had the chance to indicate his second-round control in hearts.

The Jump Shift

In days gone by, responder would jump in a new suit (a sequence such as 1◇–2♠) merely to inform partner that their side had enough for a game contract. This was an inefficient use of the call; most game-going hands are easily handled with a simple response (1◇–1♠), followed by one of the many sequences we have already seen.

Nowadays a jump shift tells partner that there is the chance of a slam. A key part of good slam bidding is to be able to suggest a slam without going past the level of game. You can then stop at a safe level when your partner is weak. In the modern style only three types are thought worthy of a jump shift:

   (i)   hands containing a powerful suit;
   (ii) certain hands of 5–3–3–2 shape;
   (iii) hands containing strong support for opener.

Strong hands which do *not* merit a jump shift are:

   (iv) balanced hands;
   (v)   two-suiters, lacking support for opener's suit.

Strong balanced hands are best described by the Baron 2 NT response, recommended in Chapter 5. Big two-suited hands are best handled with a response at the lowest level, as we shall see; you need space to describe your two-suiter and cannot afford to lose a level of bidding.

So, we recommend that you confine your jump shifts to hands of the first three types mentioned above. This style has been widely adopted in the tournament world.

Time to look at some hands. Suppose partner has opened 1♡ and you are blessed with one of these pleasing hands:

(1)   ♠ A K J 9 7 2   ♡ 5   ◇ A K 5   ♣ J 7 2

You respond 2♠. If partner rebids 3♡ you will say 3♠, letting him know that your force was based on a hand with a good suit. What if partner says 4♠ now? You will pass. That's the whole point of a jump shift; you issue your slam invitation below game level and come to rest safely when partner has an unsuitable hand.

(2)   ♠ A Q J 7 3   ♡ 9 7   ◇ A K 2   ♣ K J 9

This is the 5–3–3–2 type where a jump shift works well. Again you start with 2♠. If partner rebids 3♡ you go to 3 NT, happy that you have made your slam suggestion. (Suppose instead you respond just 1♠; your next move over 2♡ would be uncomfortable).

(3)   ♠ A 4   ♡ K J 5 3   ◇ 9 2   ♣ A K J 5 3

Partner opens 1♡ and you respond 3♣. This time the reason for your jump shift is your excellent trump support. Partner rebids 3◇ and you go to 3♡. You have made your slam suggestion; if partner can do no more than raise to 4♡, you will pass.

(4)   ♠ 10 7   ♡ 3   ◇ A K J 9 2   ♣ A K Q 5 4

This type of hand, a strong two–suiter, is not suitable for a jump shift. A start such as 1♡–3◇–3♡–4♣ would carry you too high. The auction is more comfortable after a non–jump response: 1♡–2◇–2♡–3♣. This last call is game-forcing and there is more room to investigate the best spot.

Look again at the sequence we noted above:

	West	East
	1 ♠	3 ◇
	3 ♠	4 ♣

If we can rule out the possibility that East has a two-suiter, we can assign another meaning to East's 4♣. It is a cue-bid, agreeing spades as trumps and showing the ace or king of clubs. (If East's force was based on a diamond single-suiter he would bid 4◇ at this stage, to announce his type, and possibly cue-bid the ace of clubs later.)

Here is a typical hand for the call:

(5)   ♠ K 10 4 3   ♡ 9 8   ◇ A K Q 10 5   ♣ A 4

After a start of 1♠ (from partner)–3◇–3♠, you bid 4♣. If partner's next move is 4♡, showing a heart control, you can bid Blackwood. If instead he bids just 4♠, the chances are that he has no heart control. You will pass.

The opener's rebid

Facing a jump shift, the opener rebids naturally. Since one level of bidding has already been lost, though, it is rarely right for the opener to jump again, even if he had intended to make a jump bid after a simple response.

(6)   ♠ 6 4   ♡ A K J 8 6 5   ◇ K Q 2   ♣ K 6

You open 1♡, intending to rebid 3♡ over a simple response. If partner makes a jump shift to 2♠ or 3♣, don't jump to 4♡. Save space with a 3♡ call, which will allow partner to define his hand further.

A jump by the opener has a special meaning, in fact; it shows a solid suit. Here is a complete auction involving such a bid:

West	East
♠ A K Q J 5 4	♠ 7 2
♡ 9 3	♡ A J 5
◇ Q 7 5	◇ A 9
♣ 7 2	♣ A K Q 10 4 3

West	East
1 ♠	3 ♣
4 ♠	7 ♠
End	

West's rebid is not forcing, so with another high card (even with
◇K–J–x instead of Q–x–x) he would have to rebid 3♠ for the
moment, rather than risk his partner passing 4♠.

Completing the auction

We deal with the various techniques of slam bidding in Chapter
14. Still, by way of a sneak preview, let's see a couple more
auctions that start with a jump shift.

West	East
♠ A K J 5 4	♠ 3
♡ A 2	♡ K J 4
◇ 5 3	◇ A K J 9 6 2
♣ Q J 9 4	♣ A 10 3

West	East
1 ♠	3 ◇
3 ♠	3 NT
6 NT	End

East sees that a start such as 1♠–2◇–2♠ would leave him with
an impossible call on the next round. Quite rightly he announces
his power with a jump shift. On the next round he can sit back
with a 3 NT call, content that the slam invitation has been made.

On this occasion the opener has a chunky 15–count and is happy
to advance.

West	East
♠ K 7 3	♠ A Q 10 8 6 2
♡ A J 10 5 2	♡ K 4
◇ K 5	◇ Q 4 2
♣ J 9 3	♣ A Q

West	East
1 ♡	2 ♠
3 ♠	4 ♣
4 ◇	4 NT
5 ♡	6 ♠
End	

West agrees spades and East then cue-bids in clubs (showing a
first- or second-round control – see Chapter 14). When West
subsequently shows a diamond control East embarks on Roman
Key-Card Blackwood (see Chapter 14). The 5♡ response
indicates two of the five 'aces' (♠K and ♡A) and the excellent
slam is reached.

Pre-empts at the Three- and Four-level

The tendency among many players is for non-vulnerable three-bids to become weaker and weaker, despite the fact that the potential penalties are bigger than they were a few years ago. By contrast, the standard for vulnerable three-bids has changed little over the years.

Look at the following hands. Which ones are right for a three-bid, do you think?

(1) ♠ K Q J 9 8 5 2 ♡ 5 ◇ 8 4 ♣ J 9 2

This is a typical 3♠ opener. Old-fashioned players, when vulnerable, will say, 'It's not strong enough; you might go for 800.' Most players today are more impressed by these arguments:

(a) The chance of being doubled is low when you have a good suit, particularly as most defenders use take-out doubles in the second seat.
(b) The main point of a pre-empt is to make life difficult for the opponents. It is worth some element of risk to do this.

Hand (1) is worth about 6 tricks in attack and almost nothing in defence. This means it is ideal for a pre-emptive opening.

(2) ♠ 9 5 ♡ K J 8 7 5 4 2 ◇ J 7 2 ♣ 4

Non-vulnerable, you open 3♡. Vulnerable, it's too dangerous and you have to pass for the moment.

Every pre-empt is something of a gamble; it is likely to work well when the opponents have the balance of the points, less well when you strike partner with a good hand. There are some 'rules' you may have heard which aim to make the gamble a good one, rather than a poor one. One such rule is that you should not have a 4-card major on the side.

(3)   ♠ J 8 7 3   ♡ 8   ◇ K Q 10 8 7 5 2   ♣ 7

Non-vulnerable, would you open 3◇ on this? Some pundits say not. 'What if partner has a good hand with spades?' they warn. Of course, this is a very small chance. Open 3◇ and take the blame if you miss a game in spades.

Position at the table

The odds most favour pre-emption when you are in the third position. Your partner could not open and you hold a weakish hand with little defence yourself. It doesn't take a genius to realize that things look good for the opponents. At favourable vulnerability you might open 3◇ on as little as:

(4)   ♠ 7 6   ♡ 10 7 6   ◇ K J 9 7 6 3   ♣ Q 3

Alternatively, the same call might work well on a fairly good hand, such as:

(5)   ♠ K 7 3   ♡ J 5   ◇ A K J 10 7 6   ♣ J 4

Opposite this collection your partner *might* have enough for 3 NT to make. Forget it. It's far more likely that your pre-empt will disconcert the opposition.

An opening three-bid in the fourth seat is scarcely a pre-empt in the normal sense. If you wanted to silence the opponents you could simply pass! Nevertheless a 3♣ or 3◇ opening in fourth position should not be regarded as an invitation to 3 NT. Rather it is an attempt to snatch a plus score at a point where it is unlikely your side can make a game and you want to deter an overcall.

(6) ♠ 4 ♡ A J 3 ◇ K Q 10 9 8 7 4 ♣ Q 5

Here you have the values for a one-bid. In fourth position such a call would be unattractive and you would open 3◇, trusting that this would prove too high for the other side.

Responding to Three-bids

An opening pre-empt warns you that partner's hand is unsuitable for play in any other denomination. Opposite a 3♡ or 3♠ opening, therefore, the most common question is 'Do I have enough to raise to game?' You should place partner with about six tricks in the trump suit, then work out if you are likely to make four more before the opponents can collect four tricks themselves.

(7) ♠ K 4 ♡ A K 6 ◇ Q 10 9 5 2 ♣ K 8 3

If partner opened a vulnerable 3♠ you might place him with A–Q–J–x–x–x–x and perhaps a bit of shape outside. Game is no certainty but it is a fair proposition and you are worth a raise. If the opening is non-vulnerable the prospect of ten tricks diminishes.

Suppose partner opens 3♠ and you hold:

(8) ♠ – ♡ A J 4 ◇ A K Q 10 7 5 2 ♣ Q J 5

You respond 3 NT. Such a call does not invite partner's co-operation; if he removes to 4♠ you are entitled to kick him under the table!

Over a major-suit three opening a response in a new suit at the four-level is best played as a cue-bid, with partner's suit agreed (except for 4♡ over 3♠, which is natural). Here is an auction involving such a start:

West	East
♠ A J 10 8 6 4 3	♠ K 9 2
♡ 9 5	♡ A K 3
◇ K 7 3	◇ J 8
♣ 8	♣ A K 10 9 2

West	East
3 ♠	4 ♣
4 ◇	4 NT
5 ◇	6 ♠
End	

West opens with a vulnerable 3♠ and East suggests a spade slam by cue-bidding in clubs. West's hand is suitable and he shows this with a cue-bid in diamonds. This encourages East to try Blackwood, with a happy ending.

1-star convention: Gambling 3 NT

In tournament play the traditional meaning of a 3 NT opening is that you have a solid minor with no more than the odd queen or jack outside.

(9)   ♠ Q 4   ♡ 10   ◇ A K Q J 9 7 2   ♣ 9 6 5

This is a typical 3 NT opening. In general partner will pass only when he has sufficient guards in the other suits himself.

If partner responds 4♣ he is asking to play in your minor at the four-level; you pass with clubs, correct to 4◇.

An initial response of 4◇ is conventional, asking opener to name any singleton (4 NT denies a singleton, 5 of your trump suit shows a singleton in the other minor).

West	East
♠ 4	♠ J 8 5 3
♡ J 9 2	♡ A K 8
◇ 7 5	◇ A K Q 2
♣ A K Q J 10 8 5	♣ 7 3

West	East
3 NT	4 ◇
4 ♠	6 ♣
End	

East can count 12 tricks but needs West to have a spade singleton to stop the opponents cashing two tricks there. The 4◇ 'singleton enquiry' brings forth the desired response.

Opening bids of four

4♣ and 4◇ openings (if not conventional) traditionally indicate a weak hand with a broken 8-card suit, something like:

(10)　♠ J 8 2　♡ K　◇ 5　♣ K Q 10 9 8 6 4 3

4♡ and 4♠ openings have a fairly wide range but remember that in theory they show a hand that is pre-emptive in nature. If your hand is full value for a one-bid, prefer that call.

(11)　♠ K Q 10 9 7 6 3　♡ 7 6　◇ 5　♣ K Q 9

Here you have great playing strength in spades, little defence to any enemy contract. You should therefore make a pre-emptive call and 4♠ is the right one.

In response to 4♡ or 4♠, 4NT is Blackwood and five of a new suit a cue-bid. (4♠ over 4♡ is natural, however.)

2-star convention: South African Texas

Hands suitable for natural openings of 4♣ and 4◇ occur rarely. In the South African Texas convention these calls indicate a strong major-suit pre-empt; 4♣ shows a strong 4♡ opener, 4♢ a strong 4♠ opener. The calls suggest either a solid trump suit or a one-loser suit and an ace outside.

(12)   ♠ K Q J 9 8 6 4 2   ♡ 7   ♢ A 10   ♣ J 5

You would open 4♢ on this. Make ♢A into some lesser honour and 4♠ would be the call.

Following a Texas opening, a bid of the intermediate suit (4♢ over 4♣, 4♡ over 4♢) is a slam suggestion, indicating no particular holding in the suit named.

Strong Two-bids

As we noted in Chapter 2, a strong two-bid (2◇, 2♡ or 2♠) shows a hand of power and quality, containing either one or two good suits.

(1) ♠ A K Q 7 5 2 ♡ J 10 4 ◇ – ♣ A K 9 3

Open 2♠. If you opened only 1♠ and this was passed out, you would have every reason to fear a missed game.

(2) ♠ A Q 7 6 5 ♡ A Q 9 2 ◇ A 4 ♣ K 6

This is an awkward type of hand. You must open 1♠ and hope that partner does not pass on a 1–5–4–3 type where 4♡ would be playable. If the hand were slightly stronger, say with ◇AJ, 2 NT would come into the reckoning.

The 2♣ opening

The 2♣ opening shows one of these types:

(a) a balanced hand of 23 points or more;
(b) an unbalanced hand worth game on its own, and containing at least 4½ honour tricks.

This is typical of the first category:

(3) ♠ A K 8 ♡ A Q J 5 ◇ K 6 ♣ A Q 10 4

You open 2♣. If partner responds 2◇ (negative) you rebid

2 NT, showing 23 or 24 points. Partner may pass this with a complete bust.

A 2♣ opener usually contains good defence and at least 19 points. This is an example of the second, unbalanced, type:

(4)　♠ A K J 10 3　♡ A K 5 4　♢ A Q 2　♣ 5

Open 2♣ again. You have the required number of honour tricks and would like to learn of a diamond suit opposite. The bidding might start: 2♣–2♢–2♠–3♢, leading perhaps to a slam in diamonds. If instead you were to open 2♠ and the bidding went: 2♠–2NT–3♡, partner would not expect you to be interested in a suit of five or six diamonds headed by the king.

When you have great playing strength but little defence, you should choose a strong two opening:

(5)　♠ A K Q 7 6 5　♡ K Q J 9 3　♢ –　♣ K 5

A game hand, obviously, better suited to a two-bid than to 2♣. A 2♠ opening is forcing for one round and over a negative response of 2 NT you can rebid 3♡, still forcing.

Responding to strong twos

The traditional negative response to a strong two is 2 NT; the bidding may subsequently die in three of the opener's first suit.

West	East
♠ A K J 8 5 2	♠ 7 4
♡ A 2	♡ J 9 8
♢ A K 7 4	♢ 8 5 2
♣ 3	♣ Q 10 7 5 2

West	East
2 ♠	2 NT
3 ♢	3 ♠
End	

East's values are unlikely to contribute much. Had his queen been in spades or diamonds he might have bid 4♠ at his second turn.

A positive response at the two-level is in order whenever you have a few points and a suit worth mentioning.

(6)   ♠ 6 3   ♡ K Q 10 9 3   ◇ J 2   ♣ Q 7 4 2

If partner opens 2◇ you can respond 2♡, showing the good suit. Suppose partner opens 2♠ instead; now 3♡ would consume too much space, making it harder for partner to show a 4-card club suit, for example. It would be better to start with a 2NT response; you might have a chance to show the hearts later.

When you have trump support the most enthusiastic (and convenient) response is a single raise.

(7)   ♠ 7 5   ♡ K 8 3   ◇ J 10 5 2   ♣ A Q 9 2

When partner opens 2♡ you raise to 3♡, showing good heart support, around 8 points or more, and usually one ace or two kings. With less in the way of controls you may make the less constructive direct raise to game.

(8)   ♠ Q 10 2   ♡ 6 4   ◇ Q 10 8 2   ♣ K 7 5 3

Here you raise 2♠ to 4♠. Make ♣K the ♣J and you would start with 2NT, then bid 4♠ on the next round.

1-star convention: Herbert negatives

There are two disadvantages in playing 2NT as the negative response. First, the weak hand may end up playing a notrump contract. Second, over 2◇ or 2♡ the response consumes space unnecessarily. In a scheme known as Herbert negatives the next available suit bid is used as the negative (2♡ over 2◇, 2♠ over 2♡, 3♣ over 2♠). 2NT assumes the meaning of the natural suit positive that is no longer available; for example, when partner opens 2♢ and you have a *positive* in hearts, you respond 2NT.

(3) ♠ 9 7 6 ♡ 4 2 ♢ A J 7 3 ♣ 10 5 3 2

Over 2♡ from partner you would give a Herbert negative of 2♠. Should partner rebid 2NT, another advantage of the scheme would come to light; you would raise to three and the right hand would be playing it.

Responding to 2♣

The negative response is 2♢. When you are considering a positive response in a suit, the same considerations apply as when responding to a strong two. A fair suit is enough when the response does not consume bidding space.

(10) ♠ 9 5 ♡ Q J 10 8 7 3 ♢ 10 7 ♣ K 6 2

Respond 2♡ to 2♣. Similarly if the suit were spades it would still be worth showing immediately, with a 2♠ response. Make the long suit a minor and space considerations would prevail. You would start with 2♢ and perhaps introduce the suit later, after discovering partner's type.

A 2NT response shows a balanced hand with around 9 points upwards, something like:

(11) ♠ K 10 8 7 ♡ Q 6 5 ♢ K 8 7 2 ♣ J 8

If partner were to rebid 3♡ you would simply raise to 4♡, confident that you had already indicated your values.

The 2♣ opener's rebid

When the opener rebids 2NT, showing 23–24 points, responder may pass on a bust. Otherwise he follows his normal methods opposite a 2NT opening (see Chapter 4).

A 3NT rebid shows 25–27 points. If you are ever favoured

with 28–30 points, then 4 NT would be your second call.

When the opener rebids a suit at the minimum level, this is forcing to game.

(12) ♠ A K J 10 7 ♡ A Q 6 ◇ K 6 ♣ A Q 4

After 2♣–2◇ you are not strong enough to force to game with a 2♠ rebid. Prefer 2 NT on the second round.

Completing the auction

The 2♣ opener should remember that he has already indicated a giant hand. It is sometimes difficult not to overbid good hands.

West	East
♠ A K Q 8 7	♠ 10 4
♡ A 7	♡ J 6 5 2
◇ A K Q 5	◇ 9 8 3
♣ A 4	♣ 10 8 5 2

West	East
2 ♣	2 ◇
2 ♠	2 NT
3 ◇	3 ♠
4 ♣	4 ♠

Here West has shown both his suits and been given preference to spades. His cue-bid in clubs has attracted no favourable reaction and it is time to call it a day. As you see, even 4♠ might go down on a bad day.

Turning to the responder, he should not be reluctant to show a fair suit on the second round, even though his general strength is moderate.

West	East
♠ A K 10 9 7 6	♠ 5
♡ A 9 2	♡ Q 10 8 7 5 3
♢ A K J	♢ 10 5 2
♣ A	♣ 8 7 2

West	East
2 ♣	2 ♢
2 ♠	3 ♡
4 NT[1]	5 ♣[2]
5 ♢[3]	5 NT[4]
6 ♡	End

[1] Roman Key-Card Blackwood (see Chapter 14).
[2] No key cards.
[3] Have you the queen of trumps?
[4] Yes, but no side-suit king.

East shows his heart suit on the second round (rather than bidding 2 NT, a second negative call), and a well-bid slam results.

13

Weak Two-bids

Traditionally, as we saw in the last chapter, opening two-bids show powerful hands. Most tournament players, though, like to use opening bids of 2♡ and 2♠ to show a type that occurs much more frequently: a weakish hand (about 6–10 points) containing a 6-card major. This would be typical for a weak 2♠ opening:

   (1)   ♠ K Q 10 7 5 2   ♡ 9 4   ◇ Q 8 3   ♣ 10 6

Ideally a weak two-bid should be based on a hand with most of its values in the long suit, although it's true that some tournament players treat weak twos as fire-bombs to be cast into the air at every opportunity.

   (2)   ♠ 8 3   ♡ J 9 6 5 4 2   ◇ J 4   ♣ A K 5

With only one point in the long suit and two defensive tricks outside, a weak 2♡ would give a poor picture of your hand. In our opinion it is best to maintain reasonable standards for the call.

Players who use weak two-bids need to find a different way to express hands that would otherwise qualify for a strong two-bid. One possibility is to load all such hands on to the 2♣ opener (playing that after such as 2♣–2◇–2♡–2 NT, the bidding may die in three of the opener's major). Another idea, proposed by Albert Benjamin of Scotland, has many supporters . . .

2-star convention: Benjamin two-bids

This scheme preserves the difference between hands that would normally be opened 2♣ and those worth a strong two:

2♣	A normal Acol Two in any suit (including clubs).
2♦	A normal Acol 2♣ opening.
2♥/2♠	Weak, 6–10 points.

Using this method, a sequence such as 2♣–2♦–3♣ is non-forcing. If the opener had game in his own hand he would have started with 2♦. When the 2♣ opener rebids 2♥ or 2♠, though, this is best treated as forcing up to three of the opener's major.

Responding to a weak two

When partner opens a weak two a raise to the three-level is pre-emptive; a raise to game may be pre-emptive or may be based on a good hand. Let the opponents guess!

On all weakish hands without a fit you simply pass the opening. If you are strong enough to see a chance of game you may respond along these lines:

new suit	forcing for one round;
2 NT	relay bid.

Over a 2 NT relay response partner gives further information about his hand:

3♣	6–8 points, one top trump honour;
3♦	6–8 points, two top trump honours;
3♥	8–10 points, one top trump honour;
3♠	8–10 points, two top trump honours;
3 NT	Strong trumps, KQJxxx or better.

Let's see some typical auctions triggered by a weak two.

West	East
West	*East*
♠ 8 4	♠ J 10 9 2
♡ A Q 10 8 5 2	♡ J 9 7
♢ 9 7	♢ A 10 5 3 2
♣ Q 10 3	♣ 8

West	*East*
2 ♡	3 ♡

East can judge that the opponents have a good fit somewhere, but after the raise they may end up in a bad spot.

West	*East*
♠ A Q 9 6 5 4	♠ K 10 3
♡ J 4	♡ K 9 2
♢ 10 5	♢ Q J 8 2
♣ 9 4 3	♣ A K 7

West	*East*
2 ♠	2 NT[1]
3 ♢[2]	3 NT
End	

[1] Relay.
[2] Minimum, 2 top trump honours.

East can count eight top tricks in the black suits and hopes for a ninth somewhere.

After a suit response, forcing for one round, a new suit by opener will confirm that he is not minimum.

West	East
♠ Q 5	♠ A J 9 4
♡ K J 10 7 4 2	♡ 5
◇ Q J 4	◇ K 6
♣ 8 2	♣ A K J 7 6 3

West	East
2 ♡	3 ♣
3 ◇	3 NT
End	

West, with a fair hand, shows his values in diamonds. This is enough encouragement for East to try 3 NT. If West had made the less enthusiastic rebid of 3♡, East would have passed.

West	East
♠ J 5 2	♠ 4
♡ K Q 10 8 7 2	♡ A J 3
◇ K 5	◇ A Q 9 5 4
♣ 10 3	♣ A K 6 4

West	East
2 ♡	2 NT[1]
3 ♠[2]	4 ♣[3]
4 ◇[3]	6 ♡
End	

[1] Relay, agreeing hearts.
[2] Upper range, 2 top trump honours.
[3] Cue-bids.

The good fit in two suits comes to light and East bids the slam, hoping to ruff a long card good in diamonds.

2-star convention: Multi-coloured 2◇opening

The multi-coloured 2◇ opening offers a different way to express weak-two types. Popular in Britain, it has spread to many countries. You open 2◇ on any of five different types:

(a) weak two in hearts;
(b) weak two in spades;
(c) balanced hand of 19–20 points;
(d) strong two in clubs;
(e) strong two in diamonds.

Fair enough, you will say, but how can partner find out which type you have? Initially your partner assumes you have one of the weaker types. He is likely to make one of these responses:

2♡　to play, if opener has the weak type in hearts;
2♠　to play, if opener has the weak type in spades, willing to go higher in hearts;
2NT　relay to discover the hand type.

This is a common type of auction:

West	East
♠ K Q 9 6 5 2	♠ 4
♡ 8 3	♡ A J 7 4
◇ 10 2	◇ A Q 7 4 3
♣ K 8 4	♣ Q 6 2

West	East
2 ◇	2 ♠
End	

East was willing to head for game if West had a weak two in hearts. In spades the two-level is high enough.

When responder is strong enough to contemplate game facing a weak-two type, he will usually begin with the relay bid of 2NT.

After a start of 2◇–2NT, the opener rebids like this:

3♣　upper range (8–10) weak two in hearts;
3◇　upper range (8–10) weak two in spades;
3♡　lower range (6–8) weak two in hearts;
3♠　lower range (6–8) weak two in spades.

Here is the 2 NT relay in action:

West	East
♠ 6 3	♠ A 9 4
♡ K J 9 6 5 4	♡ A 3
◇ 8 2	◇ K 10 5 4
♣ Q 10 4	♣ A 9 8 2

West	East
2 ◇	2 NT
3 ♡	End

After the 2◇ opening game looks almost certain if West has spades, quite possible if he has hearts, so East begins with a relay 2 NT. When West shows a minimum weak two in hearts, East decides to stop there.

We look briefly now at the stronger types. When the opener has a balanced 19–20 points he opens 2◇ and rebids 2 NT over 2♡ or 2♠. The bidding then proceeds as if he had opened with a normal 2 NT. In the rare case where such a 2◇ opening draws a 2 NT relay from partner, the opener will rebid 3 NT.

When the opener has the Acol two type in a minor he rebids in his suit:

West	East
♠ K Q 7	♠ J 6 5
♡ A	♡ Q 8 3 2
◇ J 7 6	◇ 9 4 3 2
♣ A K Q 10 8 6	♣ 7 5

West	East
2 ◇	2 ♡
3 ♣	End

West shows about 8 playing tricks in clubs. The call is not forcing since with a stronger hand he would have opened an Acol 2♣ rather than the multi. On this occasion East judges that his two inactive honours are insufficient for any sort of advance.

(A fuller description of the multi, and of the best defence to it, is given in *Acol in the 90s* by the present authors, published by Robert Hale.)

The multi allows you to play the traditional strong type of 2♡ and 2♠ openings while still having a means to open the more common 6–10 point types. This is the complete scheme of opening two bids:

2♣	Acol 2♣, 23+ balanced, or game-forcing hand.
2♢	Multi, as described above.
2♡/2♠	Acol strong twos.
2NT	21–22 points balanced.

The multi has its critics, but it is significant that the style has been adopted by leading players in many European countries.

14

The Art of Slam Bidding

To make a small slam you need:

  (i) the power to make 12 tricks;
 (ii) the controls to stop the defenders making 2 tricks.

The first few bids in most potential slam auctions are aimed at assessing the combined power of the two hands. When this seems to be adequate for a slam, it is time to check on controls. There are two techniques for doing this: the control-showing cue-bid and Blackwood. We look at these in turn.

The control-showing cue-bid

When a trump suit has been agreed, a bid in a new suit at the level of four or higher is a *cue-bid*, showing a control in that suit. Look at this auction:

West	East
1 ♡	1 ♠
3 ♠	4 ♣

West's 3♠ call agrees spades as trumps. East's 4♣ is therefore a cue-bid; it conveys two messages:

 (a) 'I have the ace or king of clubs, or possibly a shortage . . .
 (b) . . . and I think we may have the values for a slam.'

Cue-bids are the single most important aid to slam bidding. They invite co-operation from your partner. If he is unen-

thusiastic he will sign off; if his hand is suitable for slam purposes he will make some more encouraging move, perhaps
another cue-bid.

Note that you show the cheapest (nearest) control. Had West
cue-bid 4◇ in the auction above, he would have denied a club
control.

Let's look at some auctions involving cue-bids.

West	East
♠ A J 9 2	♠ K Q 10 6 3
♡ K 2	♡ A Q 3
◇ A K J 7 4	◇ Q 10 3
♣ J 2	♣ 8 4

West	East
1 ◇	1 ♠
3 ♠	4 ♡
4 ♠	End

East's 4♡ is a cue-bid, inviting a spade slam. It does however
deny a club control, so West signs off, despite his general
suitability for slam purposes. The power is there for a slam but
the controls are lacking.

West	East
♠ 8	♠ K Q J 10 7
♡ K Q J 7 2	♡ A 10 4 3
◇ A Q 4 3	◇ K 2
♣ A 3 2	♣ Q 8

West	East
1 ♡	2 ♠
3 ◇	3 ♡
4 ♣	4 ◇
4 NT	5 ◇
6 ♡	End

When East agrees hearts as trumps West cue-bids in clubs. East then responds with a cue-bid in diamonds. Confident now that sufficient playing strength is present for a slam, West bids Blackwood and the slam is reached. Had West held no club control, the partnership would have stopped safely in 4♡.

Cue-bidding a shortage

A side-suit void or singleton may prove just as useful as an ace or king. So you should not be shy to cue-bid such a control, particularly when you hold the hand with the shorter trump holding.

West	East
♠ A 2	♠ K J 8 2
♡ A K J 8 7 2	♡ Q 6
◇ A 10 2	◇ K J 9 8 4 3
♣ J 9	♣ 2

West	East
1 ♡	2 ◇
3 ♡	4 ♡
4 ♠	5 ♣
6 ♡	End

East cue-bids his shortage in clubs; just what West needed to hear.

In general the player with the long trumps should not cue-bid a shortage in partner's main side suit.

West	East
1 ♠	2 ♣
2 ♡	4 ♠
<u>5 ♣</u>	

If East's club suit is something like A–Q–x–x–x or K–Q–x–x–x, a singleton or void opposite is likely to be the last

88

holding he needs. When you do cue-bid in this type of auction, partner needs to be sure that you hold the ace or king, perhaps solidifying the suit.

The advance cue-bid

Sometimes a suit has not been explicitly agreed when the first cue-bid is made; the cue-bid itself agrees the suit. This is one of the most common situations:

West	East
1 NT	3 ♡
4 ♣	

West could not conceivably be introducing a club suit here. His 4♣ is a cue-bid, agreeing hearts as trumps. It indicates a good fit for hearts and a hand generally suitable for a slam, should East be that way inclined.

When a new suit call would have been forcing but instead you choose to jump in the new suit, this is usually a cue-bid.

West	East
♠ A Q 10 7 6 3	♠ K 9 5
♡ K 4 2	♡ A 4
◇ Q 4	◇ K J 9 3 2
♣ K 2	♣ A 6 5

West	East
1 ♠	2 ◇
2 ♠	4 ♣
4 ♡	5 ♡
6 ♠	End

East is too strong to bid simply 4♠ at his second turn. Instead he bids 4♣. Had he held a two-suiter in the minors he would have proceeded with 3♣, which would have been forcing. The jump to 4♣ is therefore a cue-bid, in this case agreeing spades as trumps. After two further cue-bids, the slam is reached. You can see how much better it is to exchange information in this way than to plunge into Blackwood every time you can see a slam somewhere over the hills.

However, there is a time and place for everything . . .

3-star convention: Blackwood

Following closely behind Stayman as the world's most popular convention is Blackwood. As we learnt on our mother's lap, when a trump suit has been agreed a call of 4 NT is conventional, asking how many aces partner holds. These are the traditional responses:

5♣	0 or 4 aces
5♦	1 ace
5♥	2 aces
5♠	3 aces

The time to use Blackwood is when . . .

  (i) you know you have the playing strength once you gain the lead; and

  (ii) you know that every suit is controlled.

In other words, you should use Blackwood as a final check that there are not two aces missing. Most players embark on Blackwood far too often, whenever they have 'a bit to spare' and think there might be a slam on. This is quite hopeless, of course, because partner is not being asked whether his hand is suitable for a slam, only how many aces he holds. The way to invite partner's co-operation on a slam venture is to make a cue-bid, as we have already seen.

Here is a typical *mis-use* of Blackwood:

West	East
♠ A K J 7 6 4	♠ Q 10 8 3
♡ 8	♡ A 10 9 3
◇ J 3	◇ Q 8 2
♣ A K J 2	♣ Q 8

West	East
1 ♠	3 ♠
4 NT	5 ◇
6 ♣	End

West has a fine hand, admittedly, and after his partner's double raise he is entitled to think that the values will be present for a small slam, or thereabouts. However, he cannot be sure that every suit is under control. Instead of rushing into Blackwood he should have made a cue-bid of 4♣. East's subsequent cue-bid of 4♡ would have brought to light the absence of a diamond control. (Incidentally, if West is determined to shoot for a slam he does better to bid 6♠ directly over 4♣; the Blackwood exchange gives South a chance to double the 5◇ response when he holds top cards in the suit.)

Blackwood is generally a poor idea when you hold a void. West didn't think so when this deal arose, though:

West	East
♠ A K J 8 6 5	♠ Q 10 7 3
♡ –	♡ 10 5 2
◇ K Q 10 4 2	◇ A 8 7
♣ A K	♣ 10 4 3

West	East
2 ♣	2 ◇
2 ♠	3 ♠
4 NT	5 ◇
6 ♣	End

West had no way of knowing which ace East held and the grand slam was missed. Had West made a cue-bid of 4♣ over 3♠, East would have cue-bid in diamonds, bringing the grand slam into view.

There are, in fact, relatively few hands for which Blackwood is the only check needed. This is one:

West	East
♠ 4	♠ A Q 7 6 2
♡ A K 9 8 7	♡ 6
♢ K 2	♢ 7 4
♣ A Q 8 7 2	♣ K 10 6 4 3

West	East
1 ♡	1 ♠
2 ♣	4 ♣
4 NT	5 ♢
6 ♣	End

West can see there is sufficient playing strength for a slam and every suit is under control. The response to 'old Black' indicates one ace and the good slam is reached.

If the Blackwood bidder subsequently bids 5 NT, this is a request for kings. The responses are on a similar scale:

6 ♣	0 or 4 kings
6 ♢	1 king
6 ♡	2 kings
6 ♠	3 kings

The 5 NT inquiry guarantees that all four aces are held by the partnership and, provided trump solidity is assured, responder is entitled to leap to the seven-level when he has a source of extra tricks.

2-star convention: Roman Key-Card Blackwood

The traditional responses to Blackwood are somewhat wasteful of space. Roman Key-Card Blackwood has a more effective set of responses, in which the king of the agreed trump suit counts as a fifth 'ace'. You respond to 4 NT in this way:

5♣	0 or 3 of the five 'aces';
5♢	1 or 4 of the five 'aces';
5♡	2 of the five 'aces', without the trump queen;
5♠	2 of the five 'aces', with the trump queen.

Following a 5♣ or 5♢ response, the Blackwood bidder may enquire about the trump queen by bidding the next available non-trump suit. Responder then signs off in the trump suit if he does not hold the queen of trumps, bids 5 NT or cue-bids a king otherwise.

Here are two typical sequences that make use of Roman Key-Card Blackwood:

West	East
♠ A K 9 8 2	♠ Q 10 7 5
♡ A K J 5 4	♡ 10 3
♢ 5	♢ A 9
♣ K 3	♣ A Q 8 4 2

West	East
1 ♠	2 ♣
2 ♡[1]	4 ♠
4 NT[2]	5 ♠[3]
7 ♠	End

[1] Forcing after a two-level response.
[2] Roman Key-Card Blackwood.
[3] Two 'aces' and the queen of trumps.

West	East
♠ A K J 8 7	♠ Q 10 6
♡ K Q	♡ A 9 6 3
♢ A 9	♢ 10 5 2
♣ A Q J 2	♣ K 10 6

West	East
2 ♣	2 NT
3 ♠	4 ♣[1]
4 ♢[2]	4 ♡[2]
4 NT[3]	5 ♢[4]
5 ♡[5]	6 ♣[6]
7 ♠	

[1] Cue bid, agreeing spades as trumps.
[2] Further cue bids.
[3] Roman Key-Card Blackwood.
[4] One 'ace'.
[5] Do you have the queen of trumps?
[6] Yes, and the king of clubs.

West can count 13 tricks unless East has a doubleton ace of hearts. Hoping to avoid such a cruel blow, West jumps to the grand slam.

When 4 NT is not Blackwood

4 NT is a limit bid, rather than Blackwood, when it is a raise of a natural notrump call.

(1)	West	East
	1 NT or 2 NT	4 NT

(2)	West	East
	1 NT	2 ♣
	2 ♢	4 NT

In both auctions East is asking his partner to pass with a minimum, to proceed with values to spare. 4 NT is natural also when you have previously bid 3 NT and now wish to reject an advance by partner.

	(3)	West	East
		1 ♠	2 ♦
		3 NT	4 ♦
		4 NT	End

	(4)	West	East
		1 ♦	1 ♠
		3 NT	4 ♥
		4 NT	End

In (3) West pours cold water on his partner's suggestion of a diamond slam. In auction (4) West doubtless has a fair suit of diamonds and no liking for a major-suit contract.

2-star convention: The grand slam force

A call of 5 NT, when not preceded by a Blackwood 4 NT, is a grand-slam force. It asks partner how many of the three top trump honours he holds. These are the responses:

6♣	One trump honour (0 or 1 when clubs are trumps)
6♦	A or K, plus one extra trump (when hearts or spades are trumps)
6 trump suit	No trump honour
7 trump suit	Two trump honours

This is a typical use of the call:

West	East
♠ K Q 10 7 6	♠ –
♡ A 8 7 4 2	♡ K J 10 5 3
♢ Q 4	♢ A 10 3
♣ 9	♣ A K Q 10 4

West	East
1 ♠	2 ♡
4 ♡	5 NT
6 ♢	7 ♡
End	

East uses the grand-slam force, hoping to find West with two top trump honours. West in fact responds 6♢, showing the ace or king of trumps, along with one extra trump. East judges that the grand slam is now a good investment.

15

Doubles in the Modern World

Double! Just a single word, but it has innumerable meanings at the table. Broadly speaking, there are two styles to consider: doubles of the traditional sort, as played in home games and rubber bridge in the majority of clubs; and doubles that are now standard in the tournament world.

We will look first at the basic take-out double, which is treated similarly at all forms of the game.

The values needed to double

In the second seat you may double on no more than 11 points or so, if you have good support for all the unbid suits.

 (1) ♠ K 10 7 6 ♡ A 9 3 ◇ 9 ♣ K J 9 3 2

This is an acceptable double of 1◇ when non-vulnerable. Add another jack or so and you would make the call vulnerable. 5–4–3–1 is a particularly good shape for a take-out double, better than the much vaunted 4–4–4–1.

 It is not clever to double on weaker hands.

 (2) ♠ J 8 6 4 ♡ – ◇ K 9 6 2 ♣ A 10 7 4 3

You will meet players who double 1♡ on this, claiming that they are prepared for any response. Sometimes partners respond in notrumps, though, which is hopeless for this hand; sometimes they would prefer to defend against an enemy contract in hearts, and sometimes they will double the opponents too soon.

When an opening one-bid is followed by two passes the standards for a double are lowered. There is now a strong presumption that your side has the balance of the cards. After 1♥–No–No, you should double on as little as:

(3)   ♠ Q J 9 8   ♡ 8 4   ◇ A J 5 2   ♣ J 10 7

The situation would be different if the opening bid on your left had been 1◇ or 1♠. You might reasonably think that you had good defence against either of these; also, partner is unlikely to have passed on a good hand with strength in the enemy suit. The effect of doubling might be to jockey the opponents into a better fit in hearts.

It is particularly important to compete when the opponents have found a fit, yet have stopped at a low level. This type of sequence is very common:

Love-all, dealer South

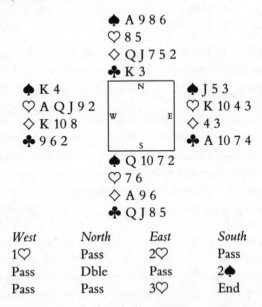

West	North	East	South
1♡	Pass	2♡	Pass
Pass	Dble	Pass	2♠
Pass	Pass	3♡	End

When the bidding returns to North in 2♡ he can be sure that his partner must have a fair number of points. Although North passed over 1♡, his double of 2♡ is unquestionably for take-out. Having successfully pushed the opponents to the three-level, North-South must not commit the *faux pas* of competing further with 3♠ ('It looked as though we had found a fit, partner'). That is one of the surest ways of transforming a plus into a minus.

Can a player who has made a simple overcall in a suit subsequently double for take-out? Yes, indeed. Look at this sequence:

West	North	East	South
1♡	1♠	2♡	No
No	Dble		

Again the opponents have stopped low with a fit. North will not want to lie down and die on a hand such as:

(4) ♠ A K 10 8 5   ♡ 7 2   ◇ K J 7   ♣ K 10 8

The double invites South to pick a suit.

When the opponents have bid two suits, and especially when there has been a response at the two-level, you should almost always wait to see which way things are going.

(5) ♠ 7 2   ♡ A Q J 2   ◇ 10 3   ♣ K Q 10 5 2

After a start of 1♠–Pass–2◇–? it may well be that your partner is very weak, and it would be foolish to double. Pass now; if opener re-bids 2♠ and this comes round to you, a double (for take-out) is tempting. Remember this general point: if you stay silent with a good hand throughout the bidding, the opponents will surely misplace the lie of the cards at some point. The detective in plain clothes is not so conspicuous as the policeman in uniform.

Responding to a take-out double

The bidding begins:

West	North	East	South
1♦	Dble	No	?

When considering your response, distribution is as important as high-card points. That proviso made, we suggest this general guide to responses:

minimum suit bid	0–8 points;
jump in suit	8–10 points;
1 NT	5–9 points, with good stop in the enemy suit;
2 NT	10–11 points;
3 NT	12 or more points;
cue-bid	11 points or more, where the best denomination is in doubt.

We look first at responding on weak hands. Suppose the bidding has started:

West	North	East	South
1♦	Dble	Pass	?

You might hold:

(6)   ♠ J 2   ♡ 10 8 5 2   ♦ K 3   ♣ 9 7 6 5 4

Respond 1♡. Your clubs are longer but on such a weak hand it is best to make a cheap response. In any case partner is usually more interested to hear of a major suit than a minor.

(7)   ♠ 9 5   ♡ Q 10 3   ♦ J 9 5 4 2   ♣ J 6 3

You are not strong enough for a 1 NT response. Nor are your diamonds anywhere near good enough for a penalty pass. Best is to bid 1♡, again, keeping the bidding low.

On hand (7) you had a *little* support for hearts, so it was safe to bid a 3-card suit. Suppose you had to find a response on this unfortunate collection, though:

(8)   ♠ 10 7 2   ♡ 8 6 5   ◇ Q 9 7 2   ♣ 9 6 3

Now 2♣ is less likely to lead to a calamity than any of the grisly alternatives. (It is wrong to think that 1♡ is safer; it is much more likely to attract an unwelcome raise.)

(9)   ♠ 8 4   ♡ A Q J 2   ◇ 10 7 3   ♣ J 9 5 2

Since a 1♡ response guarantees no strength whatsoever, some players feel obliged to jump to 2♡ on this type of hand. This is quite unnecessary. If partner has 16 or 17 points and good heart support, he will raise your 1♡ response to 2♡. Then you will have enough, but only just enough, to go to 4♡.

Next we look at hands in the middle range, where a jump response is justified.

(10)   ♠ 10 3   ♡ A Q 9 7 2   ◇ K 5 2   ♣ 9 7 4

If partner doubles 1♣ or 1◇, you respond 2♡. This is a limited call and partner may pass. Should he instead introduce a new suit, this would be forcing for one round. Had partner doubled 1♠, you would have had little room in which to express your values and would be well worth a jump to 3♡.

(11)   ♠ Q 10 6 2   ♡ 7 3   ◇ 8 6   ♣ A Q 7 5 2

If partner doubles one of a red suit you are worth a jump response. It is a close decision whether to bid 2♠, showing the major, or 3♣, hoping that there will be further bidding and that you will be able to mention the spades later.

When you hold the values for game or thereabouts, but no particularly long suit, you start with a cue-bid in the opponent's suit:

(12) ♠ A Q 10 2   ♥ K 9 3 2   ♦ Q 9 7   ♣ 5 4

When partner doubles 1♦ you show your strength with a cue-bid of 2♦. This is not forcing to game but it is 'forcing to suit agreement'. On this hand, if your partner's next bid is 2♥ or 2♠ you will give him a single raise; the bidding may die there.

(13) ♠ A Q 10 8 5 4   ♥ 5   ♦ 8 3   ♣ A 5 4 2

Again suppose partner has doubled 1♦. There is some chance of a slam here and you are too strong to jump straight to 4♠. Start with a cue-bid of 2♦, then jump in spades on the next round.

Responding to a double after interference

When the third player names a major suit over your partner's double you must bear in mind that he may be playing games.

West	North	East	South
1♦	Dble	1♠	?

(14) ♠ A J 8 7   ♥ K 6   ♦ 10 8 3   ♣ 9 7 4 2

Since your partner is likely to have some length in spades, it may well be that the 1♠ intervention is a bluff. You should double, for penalties, saying no more than that you would have bid 1♠ had East passed.

(15) ♠ 9 3   ♥ Q 10 2   ♦ A J 10 5   ♣ J 6 3 2

Here you indicate your moderate values with a call of 1 NT. You hold the diamonds strongly and partner will doubtless have something good in spades.

When the third player redoubles

Suppose the bidding starts like this:

West	North	East	South
1◇	Dble	Rdble	?

South is not obliged to bid now and would pass on such as:

(16)   ♠ 10 4 2   ♡ Q 7 6   ◇ 8 3 2   ♣ J 5 4 3

However, a bid by South in this position would not in any way be strength-showing.

(17)   ♠ 4 3   ♡ Q 8 7 4   ◇ J 6 3 2   ♣ 7 4 3

On this it would be sensible to bid 1♡, to save partner from impaling himself in 1♠ or 2♣.

All positive calls by fourth hand, such as a jump bid in a suit or a cue-bid, are value-showing; otherwise there is no way to show a good hand.

We turn now to occasions where in the tournament world a double has not quite the same meaning as at rubber bridge. The first example, in its simplest form, is perhaps on the borderline, since many rubber-bridge players would treat it in the same way.

2-star convention: Responsive doubles

While the general rule is that a double is for penalties when partner has bid or doubled, an exception occurs when partner has made a take-out double and the next player has raised. This is the simplest situation:

West	North	East	South
1♡	Dble	2♡	Dble

South is not doubling for penalties but to show values and encourage his partner to take some action. The meaning would be the same if East had raised to 3♡.

Here is a complete deal illustrating the technique:

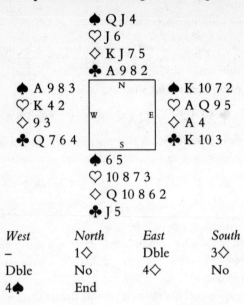

West	North	East	South
–	1◇	Dble	3◇
Dble	No	4◇	No
4♠	End		

If East at his second turn made a call such as 3♡, this would not be forcing. He shows his strength with a cue-bid and the best contract is reached.

At what point does a responsive double merge into a penalty double? The conservative answer (of which we approve) is when 3♠ is doubled. Some pundits, when answering problems in the magazines, carry the idea to a much higher level, declaring that 1♠–Dble–4♠–Dble is responsive. Presumably they hold better cards than the rest of us!

2-star convention: Competitive doubles

It is rarely productive to double the opponents at a low level when they have found a fit. What better use can be made of a double, then, in an auction such as this:

West	North	East	South
1♡	1♠	2♡	Dble

Under a scheme known as 'competitive doubles', South's double is for take-out. It shows good values in the unbid suits and some tolerance, usually a doubleton, for partner's suit. This would be a typical hand for the bid:

(18) ♠ 10 6   ♡ 7   ♢ Q 10 8 7 5   ♣ A J 9 3 2

Where the opponents have found a fit all doubles up to the level of 3♡ carry the same meaning: 'I have the values for a bid but no good bid to make'. The bid may be used by the opening side too:

West	North	East	South
1♢	1♡	1♠	2♡
Dble			

Again, West's double is not for penalties. It indicates a desire to compete but leaves the choice of suit to partner.

Penalty doubles

All doubles by the side that has opened 1 NT are for penalties. A double by the defending side after a 1 NT opening is normally for penalties too, but there are some sequences where it will look as though the doubler wants to hear from his partner. For example:

West	North	East	South
1 NT	No	2♡	No
No	Dble		

Here the opponents are limited and the natural assumption is that North proposes to compete, perhaps with something like:

(19) ♠ A 10 8 6   ♡ 7   ♢ K 10 9 6 5   ♣ K J 4

Relatively few low-level doubles are now played for penalties. In social and rubber bridge this type of auction is perhaps the largest source of penalty doubles:

West	North	East	South
1♠	2♢	Dble	

In tournament play, though, such a call would normally be a 'negative double', for take-out (see Chapter 17).

A double of a 1NT opening is for penalties, as are any subsequent doubles in an auction like this:

West	North	East	South
1NT	Dble	2♡	Pass
Pass	Dble		

North's second double is for penalties too, although it may be based more on points rather than a stack of trumps.

Most doubles of game contracts are for penalties. A double of a heart game, when it is the doubler's first chance to bid, will indicate fair support for spades.

West	North	East	South
1♡	Pass	4♡	Dble

North will pass the double for penalties when he holds a bust. He should take it that South will not be averse to a 4♠ contract, though, should North himself hold some length there.

Most players treat this double for penalties:

West	North	East	South
1♡	Pass	1♠	Pass
2♡	Dble		

North is assumed to hold a stack of hearts and good values. Had he wished to compete in the minors at this stage, he could have bid an unusual 2NT, anyway.

Lead-directing doubles

When the opponents are in the middle of a constructive auction you should remain alert for the chance to make a lead-directing double, perhaps of some artificial bid.

West	North	East	South
1♠	Pass	2♣	Pass
2♦	Pass	2♡	Dble

East makes an artificial call in the fourth suit and South doubles to let North know that he would like a heart lead.

In slam auctions you often have the opportunity to double a cue-bid or a Blackwood response.

West	North	East	South
1♠	Pass	3♦	Pass
3♠	Pass	4♠	Pass
4 NT	Pass	5♡	Dble

Again South is suggesting that a heart lead may be worthy of consideration. Equally important – if South does *not* double 5♡ there will usually be some other lead he would prefer.

3-star convention: Lightner double

It is a waste of time to play doubles of a freely-bid slam merely for penalties. Suppose you do make a penalty double, holding two aces, and both the aces stand up. You have scored 100 instead of 50; what use is that? It was a disaster for the opponents anyway.

Even at rubber bridge it is almost universal to play doubles of freely bid slams as lead-directing, perhaps suggesting a void somewhere. Suppose you are West on this auction:

West	North	East	South
–	–	–	1♠
Pass	3♠	Pass	4 NT
Pass	5♦	Pass	6♠
Pass	Pass	Dble	End

You have to find a lead from this collection:

(20) ♠ 9 7 ♡ J 9 7 6 4 3 ♦ J 10 9 ♣ Q 4

Without a double you would doubtless have led ♦J. After the Lightner double your choice will be a heart. It doesn't need a fortune-teller to predict a heart void in partner's hand.

16

All about Overcalls

Your right-hand opponent opens 1♣ and you overcall 1♠, perhaps on a hand such as:

(1)   ♠ A Q 10 9 4   ♡ 10 3   ◇ Q 7 6   ♣ 8 5 2

What are the potential advantages of such a call? There are several:

(a) You rob the opponents of bidding space (here the respon-
     der cannot bid 1◇ or 1♡ and may not be happy to bid
     1 NT);
(b) You suggest a good opening lead to partner;
(c) You may reach a playable contract or a worthwhile
     sacrifice.

The overcall on hand (1) was justified on all three counts given above, even though the hand contained only 8 points, well short of the values for an opening bid.

Suppose instead that the opponents open 1♠ and you hold this collection:

(2)   ♠ Q 9 4   ♡ 6 3   ◇ A Q 3   ♣ A 10 5 3 2

Although you hold more points here – the values for an opening bid, in fact – the hand is not worth an overcall of 2♣. Look back at the three criteria we noted above. A 2♣ overcall would not consume much space, nor would it necessarily indicate the best lead. More importantly, you might concede a large penalty by overcalling 2♣. The suit is poor and the overcall is at the two-level. Give partner a weak hand with one or two small clubs and the penalty might run to four figures.

What strength is needed to overcall?

As we saw in the two example hands above, it is more important to have a good suit and fair playing strength than to hold a certain number of points. Most one-level overcalls fall into the 8–13 point range; two-level overcalls show more like 10–14.

Suppose the player on your right opens 1$\diamondsuit$. Would you overcall on any of these hands:

(3) ♠ K Q 10 8 5   ♡ 6 $\diamondsuit$ 10 7 3 2   ♣ K 5 2

Non-vulnerable you should certainly call 1♠. It is always tempting to get spades, the senior suit, into the auction. Here you will make it more difficult for the opponents to discover a heart fit. If your suit was hearts instead of spades there would be less reason to overcall 1♡.

(4) ♠ Q 8 7 6 2   ♡ K J 5 $\diamondsuit$ 7 4   ♣ A 8 2

Here you pass. You have two points more than on the previous hand but your spades are weak and you should not insist on a spade lead. Suppose the bidding went 1$\diamondsuit$–1♠–3NT. You would be worried that partner, with a fair club or heart suit, would lead from two or three small spades.

(5) ♠ A K J 4   ♡ 8 2 $\diamondsuit$ Q 9 3   ♣ A 10 5 2

Bid 1♠. When you have plenty of points, but the wrong shape for a take-out double, it is quite acceptable to overcall in a strong 4-card suit at the one-level. Otherwise you might find yourself shut out of the auction. (Rixi Markus, one might remark, seldom hesitated to introduce a 4-card suit at the *four*-level!)

Jump overcalls

The traditional jump overcall is stronger than a simple overcall. It suggests opening values, about 12–15 points, and usually a 6-card suit.

    (6)   ♠ A Q J 9 6 2   ♡ Q 8 3   ◇ K J 4   ♣ 7

Bid 2♠ over one of a suit. The fact that such jump overcalls are available on a hand of this type provides a useful limitation to the strength of a simple overcall. When partner overcalls 1♠ you don't have to keep the bidding open on some moderate 9-count ('in case you had a big hand, partner').

A three-level jump overcall in a minor will turn partner's sights towards 3 NT and should therefore be based on a good suit. Look at these two hands:

    (7)   ♠ 10 4   ♡ J 10 3   ◇ A 5   ♣ A K J 10 7 6

    (8)   ♠ A K 4   ♡ 8 2   ◇ K 7   ♣ K 10 7 6 4 3

Bid 3♣ (over any suit bid) on (7) but only 2♣ on (8). The second hand will not provide a game unless partner has a good club holding. In that case he will doubtless make some move, such as raising the clubs.

1-star convention: Weak jump overcalls

More in sorrow than in anger, we have to record that in the tournament world many players favour weak jump overcalls. Over an opening of 1◇ a non-vulnerable jump to 2♠ might be made on as little as:

    (9)   ♠ A Q 9 8 3   ♡ 7 6   ◇ J 7 4   ♣ 10 9 2

This is not the recommended style of the authors, but we wish the exponents of this method well.

Responding to overcalls

In competitive auctions it pays to raise partner freely when you have trump support. Even if you go one or two down you will find that the opponents had a good fit somewhere and could have made a contract themselves (they are both relatively short in your suit, so are bound to have matching length somewhere).

Suppose your partner overcalls 1♠ in an auction such as 1◇–1♠–Pass. What would you do with this hand:

(10) ♠ K 10 4   ♡ J 8 2   ◇ 6 4   ♣ K 10 7 5 2

Raise to 2♠. Your hand does not amount to much and game is certainly a distant prospect. By raising, though, you deprive the opener of space. You also let partner know that a spade lead will be welcome.

(11) ♠ A 10 7 4   ♡ 5   ◇ 8 7 2   ♣ Q 10 9 5 3

Here you would raise pre-emptively to 3♠, cramping the opener even more.

If such direct raises are pre-emptive, what do you do on a hand with more points, one worth a genuine game try? Again the auction starts 1◇–1♠–Pass and you hold:

(12) ♠ A 10 5   ♡ K Q 8   ◇ 6 5 2   ♣ K 10 9 3

On this type of hand you make a cue-bid in the opponent's suit, here 2◇. This means initially 'I have a high-card raise of your suit to at least the two-level.' If partner has a minimum overcall he will rebid 2♠ (which on this hand you would pass); otherwise he will make a more constructive call. The cue-bid suggests that you hold some defence, as well as trump support. It allows partner to judge the subsequent auction more accurately.

Since an overcall indicates fair playing strength, there is little point in 'rescuing' partner into another suit. Even though you might occasionally wish to do this, it is better in the long run to play that a change-of-suit call is constructive. Some partnerships play that a bid in a new suit is forcing, but in our opinion that is overdoing it.

The bidding starts 1♡–1♠–Pass. Do you move on this:

(13)   ♠ 8 5   ♡ 7 6   ◇ Q 10 5   ♣ A Q 10 9 7 2

Pass. You are not strong enough for a constructive move. Remember that partner's one-level overcall doesn't promise the earth. Make ◇Q into ◇A and you are worth 2♣. If you were appreciably stronger with long clubs, then you would have to call 3♣, since 2♣ is non-forcing. A cue-bid of 2♡, remember, would imply support for partner's suit.

Responses in notrumps are limit bids, made on the assumption that partner is minimum for his call. If partner has overcalled at the one-level, this would be the scale:

1 NT	about 10–12 points;
2 NT	about 13–14 points;
3 NT	15 points or more.

Few things are more annoying than for partner to leap to 3 NT on some nondescript 13-count and then, when he has gone down, say 'Yes, well, you only had 9 points for your 1♠ overcall'.

An overcall at the two-level suggests more serious values and you may try for a notrump game on correspondingly less.

2 NT	about 10–12 points;
3 NT	13 points or more.

Points are not everything in this area. An honour in partner's long suit, or a double stop in the opponent's suit, will be encouraging factors. Q–10–9–x is more likely to provide a double stop than such as A–8–x–x, for example.

Let's see a couple of complete auctions.

	West		East
	♠ A J 9 6 5		♠ K Q 4
	♡ Q J 9 4		♡ 8 2
	◇ J 6		◇ Q 10 7 3
	♣ K 7		♣ A Q 8 2

North–South game

West	North	East	South
–	–	–	1♡
1♠	Pass	2♡	Pass
2NT	Pass	3NT	End

East's 2♡ cue-bid suggests a sound raise to at least two spades. With a moderate overcall West would sign off in 2♠. Here he has a respectable hand and makes the more constructive call of 2NT. This suits East admirably and he raises to game.

	West		East
	♠ K Q 10 7 6 2		♠ 8 4
	♡ Q 4		♡ K J 7 3
	◇ J 8 6		◇ K Q 5 2
	♣ 7 5		♣ A 9 4

West	North	East	South
–	–	–	1◇
1♠	Pass	1NT	Pass
2♠	End		

East bids only 1NT, realizing that his partner's values may be limited. West confirms this with his 2♠ rebid and the partnership stops at a safe level.

1NT overcall

A 1NT overcall in the second position (an auction beginning 1♡–1NT) should show good values, about 15–17 points. Suppose you hold this hand:

(14)   ♠ K Q 7 ♡ K 2 ◇ A J 8 7 ♣ K J 9 3

This makes a fine 1 NT overcall over 1♣, 1◇ or 1♠. Over 1♡ a double would be better.

In the fourth position (in an auction such as 1♠–Pass–Pass–1 NT), 1 NT is usually played as about 11–14 points. With more than that you would start with a double.

(15)   ♠ A 10 7 ♡ K 7 ◇ K 10 7 6 ♣ J 9 3 2

If 1♠ is passed round to you, compete with 1 NT. It's likely that the points are fairly even between the two sides, so you don't want to let the opponents choose trumps. Apart from that, partners do occasionally have 13 points or so; you might have a game on. At duplicate, players often make such a call without a stopper in the opener's suit.

Responding to a 1 NT overcall

When your partner overcalls 1 NT, either in the 2nd or 4th position, you follow the same course as when facing a 1 NT opening. Rubber bridge players will play natural responses, including weak take-outs. Duplicate players will play 2♣ as Stayman and other responses as transfers; (an exception is a sequence such as 1♡–1 NT–Pass–2◇; since there would be little point in a transfer into opener's suit, 2◇ is natural).

Two-suited overcalls

We look now at the best way to enter the auction when the opponents have opened with one of a suit and you hold a pronounced two-suiter elsewhere. Suppose the player to your right has opened 1♡ and you hold a hand of this type:

(16)   ♠ 2 ♡ K 2 ◇ K Q J 9 8 ♣ Q J 10 4 2

You can hardly double, with only a singleton in spades. In the absence of any convention you would have to overcall 2◇, intending perhaps to bid 3♣ on the next round. It is better, though, to look for some conventional means to indicate both suits at one go. There are two conventions that are widely played here and we look at them in turn.

2-star convention: Unusual Notrump

Overcalls of 2 NT in the second position (such as 1♡–2 NT), and any notrump calls that cannot logically show a strong balanced hand, are conventional; they indicate a two-suiter in the two lowest unbid suits. So, playing this scheme, you would overcall 2 NT on hand (16), above.

Some players use this convention far too much, entering the auction on any flimsy two-suiter. This is silly. Even with fairly good suits you may run into a large penalty. Also, whenever you make such a call and the opponents end up playing the hand, you will have given them valuable information.

Apart from direct overcalls of 2 NT there are many other opportunities to make 'unusual notrump' calls. Suppose your right-hand opponent opens 1♠ and you hold this hand:

(17) ♠ A 2   ♡ 10   ◇ K J 8 7   ♣ A Q 10 8 4 2

You overcall 2♣; the next player raises his partner to 2♠, and this call runs back to you. Your hand justifies further competition and the best call now is 2 NT. Obviously this cannot show a strong balanced hand since you made a 2♣ overcall on the previous round. Partner will read it as 'unusual', showing a desire to compete in one or other of the lowest two suits.

The Unusual Notrump convention, at any rate in its simpler forms, is widely played even at rubber bridge.

2-star convention: Michaels cue-bid

In this convention a cue-bid in the opponent's suit shows a two-suiter that includes both major suits or the unbid major suit. So, 2♢ over 1♢ (or 2♣ over 1♣) shows both majors. 2♡ over 1♡ shows a two-suiter including spades; 2♠ over 1♠ shows a two-suiter including hearts.

These cue-bids do not promise a particularly strong hand. Non-vulnerable you might make a Michaels call on about 9 points upwards.

Suppose there is a 1♢ opening in front of you and you hold:

(18)   ♠ K 8 7 5 3   ♡ K J 9 4 2   ♢ Q 2   ♣ 8

In the absence of any convention you would have to overcall 1♠, perhaps showing the hearts later. Playing Michaels, you can show the type immediately with an overcall of 2♢.

A Michaels call in a major will often push the bidding to the three-level, so should be based on correspondingly sounder values. Over 1♠ this would represent a minimum Michaels 2♠ overcall, non-vulnerable:

(19)   ♠ 2   ♡ A Q 9 8 2   ♢ K J 10 9 2   ♣ Q 2

When partner has no fit for the other major, hearts in this case, he may bid 2 NT. This is conventional and asks you to show your minor suit.

Michaels cue-bids are used mainly in tournament play. At rubber bridge the overcall more often displays the traditional type, a super take-out double.

17

Responding after Intervention

As we saw in Chapter 16, one of the reasons for overcalling is to prevent certain calls by the player to your left. In this chapter we will see how third hand should act after the intervention.

We will cover in turn the tactics over a double and over a bid.

When the second hand has doubled

How would you interpret East's bid in this sequence:

West	North	East	South
1◇	Dble	1♠	

There are two possible answers. Traditionally East's bid is non-forcing; it promises no values and may well be a rescue bid on a hand that has no liking for a 'one diamond doubled' contract.

In the cauldron of the tournament world it was realized long ago that this was not the best use of the bid. First of all, it is very unusual for a take-out double of a one-bid to be left in for penalties. Secondly, when such a double is passed by the fourth player the opener will be fully aware of the trump stack to his right. He can instigate a rescue operation himself. So, in tournament bridge a different method has been widely adopted . . .

2-star convention: Ignoring the double

This might perhaps be described as a treatment rather than a convention. The idea is that any change of suit by responder carries the same meaning over a double as it would without a double. In a sequence such as 1♡–Dble–1♠, the 1♠ call is forcing (unless responder has already passed).

Suppose that after 1◇(from partner)–Dble you are looking at:

   (1)   ♠ A Q 9 5 4   ♡ 8 3   ◇ K 10 4   ♣ Q 8 2

Playing standard methods you cannot bid 1♠, since it is non-forcing and may be merely a rescue. You therefore have to start with a strength-showing redouble (even though you know that the opponents have a bolt-hole in 1♡). The auction flows more smoothly if you 'ignore the double' and bid a forcing 1♠.

Sometimes a double by second hand will incline you to one action rather than another. After 1♡–Dble you hold:

   (2)   ♠ Q 10 3 2   ♡ 7 5   ◇ K 9 7   ♣ A 8 5 4

Without the double you would respond 1♠ in case partner held the spades with you. Here the doubler has suggested good spades, so 1 NT is a better call on your hand. This shows 7–9 points over a double.

When you have a fit for partner

When your partner's suit opening is doubled and you have good trump support for him, it is well known that you should raise him to the limit, attempting to make life difficult for fourth hand. After 1♡–Dble you hold:

   (3)   ♠ 10 8 4   ♡ K 10 7 5   ◇ 7   ♣ J 10 6 3 2

You raise to 3♡, one more than you would bid without the intervening double.

Since a raise to 3♡ is pre-emptive over a double you must find a different call when you have a sound raise to the three-level. The time-honoured answer is to bid 2 NT; this could hardly be natural, since you would redouble with a balanced 11-count.

The redouble

In an auction such as 1♠–Dble–Rdble, the redouble tells partner that your side has the balance of the points. On many occasions it will lead to a penalty double.

On most hands the opener will run the fourth player's bid back to the redoubler, in case he wants to apply the axe. Only when the opener is disinterested in penalizing the opponents' contract *and* holds a weak hand himself should he bid in front of his partner.

(4)   ♠ K 10 9 8 7 2   ♡ A 9 8   ◇ 6   ♣ Q J 6

After 1♠–Dble–Rdble–2◇ you bid 2♠ immediately. This warns partner of a minimum hand unsuited to a penalty double. Add in one more honour, such as ♡Q, and you would pass over 2◇, intending to revert to spades later.

Note that the redoubler promises another bid if the auction returns to him. If he introduces a new suit, this will be forcing for one round.

When there has been an overcall

Your partner opens 1♣ and the next player overcalls 1♠. Traditional methods for the responder are that a double is for penalties and a new suit is forcing (unless responder has already passed). How often will you have a worthwhile penalty double of 1♠, though? It will almost always be simpler, and more rewarding, to play in 3 NT your way.

Quite rightly the troops of the tournament world have adopted a different, and much more effective, meaning for such doubles by responder . . .

3-star convention: Negative doubles

When the bidding starts with one of a suit, followed by a natural overcall (up to the level of 3♡), a double by the third player is for *take-out*. Such a double is known as a 'negative double' and carries two messages:

(a) 'I have the values to bid . . .
(b) . . . but no good bid to make.'

Such a double suggests 4-card holdings in the unbid suits, particularly any unbid major, but does not guarantee this. The opener will make his rebid on the assumption that responder has a flattish hand of around 8–10 points. If the responder is in fact stronger, this will become apparent at his next turn.

Suppose partner opens 1♣, the next player bids 1♠, and you are looking at:

(5)　♠ 10 5 2　♡ A J 7 3　♢ K 10 4 2　♣ Q 6

Using standard methods, you would have to call 2♢, which is hardly ideal. A negative double expresses the hand admirably, though. On this occasion you have 4-card holdings in both the unbid suits and no continuation by partner will prove unwelcome.

Some players restrict the use of negative doubles solely to overcalls of 1♠. Most players use them much more freely, often up to the level of 3♡ or 3♠. It might seem that you will lose out on the opportunity to collect penalties, but this does not happen in practice. Suppose you find yourself in this situation . . . partner opens 1♡, the next player bids 2♣, and you hold:

(6)　♠ A Q 4　♡ 9 2　♢ 10 8 7 6　♣ Q J 9 4

A double would (unfortunately, in this case) be for take-out. You therefore do best to pass. If the bidding returns to your partner he will realize that you may have a hand of this type, particularly as the fourth player has not ventured a raise. Much of the time, then, your partner will reopen the bidding with a take-out double, which you will be happy to pass. Some players go so far as to say that they will always reopen in this type of situation, unless they themselves hold length in the suit of the overcall.

Even though the use of negative doubles is almost universal in tournament play, there is still much disagreement about sequences such as these:

	West	North	East	South
(i)	1♢	1♠	2♣	
(ii)	1♢	1♠	2♡	

Should 2♣ in (i) and 2♡ in (ii) be forcing? To play them forcing gives you more accuracy on game-going hands. To play them non-forcing allows you to compete more freely on weakish hands.

Most players treat 2♣ in (i) as forcing, since no space has been lost. Where space has been lost, as in (ii), it makes good sense to play such bids as non-forcing.

When you are strong and (in sequence ii) want to force, you can always begin with a negative double and introduce your hearts on the next round. This sequence is forcing. Suppose partner opens 1♢ and there is a 1♠ overcall. You hold:

(7)   ♠ A 2   ♡ K J 10 8 7 2   ♢ 9 3   ♣ 10 6 5

This hand is ideal for the '2♡ non-forcing' style. Add in the ♣A and you will have to double first and introduce the hearts on the next round.

18

Intervention over 1 NT

When the opponents open a weak notrump, any range between 10–12 and 14–16, this is the traditional defence:

Double   For penalties, 15 points or more.
2♣/2◇/2♡/2♠   Natural overcall, about 11–14 points.

The method is the same whether the left-hand or right-hand opponent made the opening call.

     (1)   ♠ A Q 9 7 6 2   ♡ 6   ◇ K J 3   ♣ A K 4

Over 1 NT you double, for penalties.

When partner's 1 NT is doubled

Suppose partner opens a 12–14 1 NT and the next player doubles. What do you say on this?

     (2)   ♠ 9 6 4   ♡ J 9 5 2   ◇ 7   ♣ Q 10 8 5 2

1 NT doubled may be expensive, so you run to 2♣ (natural, not Stayman). Other escapes, such as 2◇ or 2♡ are also natural, even when without the double they would have been transfer responses.

    Suppose, after the same start, you have a better hand:

     (3)   ♠ K 10 8 5 2   ♡ 4   ◇ K J 5 2   ♣ J 9 3

Now your side has at least half the points in the pack and you may fancy your chances in 1 NT doubled. It is dangerous to pass, though, because the doubler may have a long string of hearts, or even clubs. In the long run it is better to enter with 2♠; for one thing, you may prevent them getting together in hearts.

Suppose you are even stronger:

    (4)   ♠ K 9 5 4   ♡ A 10 6   ◇ J 4   ♣ Q 9 3 2

Now, too, it would be a mistake to pass. Some players would, saying '1 NT doubled and made with an overtrick or two will be a good score'. Much more likely is that the fourth player will take out to 2◇. If this runs back to you, what will you do then? The answer on hands of this type is to redouble on the first round, telling partner that your side has a clear majority of the points. This gives him the chance to double any retreat by the fourth player.

When partner doubles 1 NT

When the bidding starts 1 NT–Dble–Pass, the first point to remember is that partner is not asking you to bid. His double is intended for penalties. You might hold:

    (5)   ♠ 10 5   ♡ 8 4 3   ◇ Q 9 5 4 2   ♣ K J 6

Don't take out to 2◇. You have 6 points and partner has at least 15, maybe more. You should therefore pass and hope to take a worthwhile penalty. Make ♣K into a small club and you might then remove the double to 2◇. Even then, it could well be the wrong decision.

When your partner doubles 1 NT and you see a fair chance for game your way, this may be an easier way to make a living than defending 1 NT.

    (6)   ♠ K Q 10 8 5 2   ♡ 6 2   ◇ Q 7 5 3   ♣ 10

Here you would invite game with a jump to 3♠. Strengthen the diamonds by a point or two and you would bid 4♠.

This is a complete auction starting with a double of 1 NT:

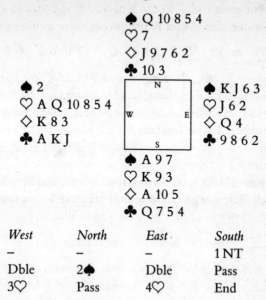

	♠ Q 10 8 5 4	
	♡ 7	
	◇ J 9 7 6 2	
	♣ 10 3	
♠ 2		♠ K J 6 3
♡ A Q 10 8 5 4		♡ J 6 2
◇ K 8 3		◇ Q 4
♣ A K J		♣ 9 8 6 2
	♠ A 9 7	
	♡ K 9 3	
	◇ A 10 5	
	♣ Q 7 5 4	

West	*North*	*East*	*South*
–	–	–	1 NT
Dble	2♠	Dble	Pass
3♡	Pass	4♡	End

North takes refuge in spades and is doubled by East. West's unbalanced hand is unsuitable for defence, so he goes to 3♡. This is not forcing but East has enough to raise to game.

2-star convention: Two-suited overcalls of 1 NT

Natural overcalls of 2♣ and 2◇ are not of much value. You are a long way from game and the opposition can usually outbid you in the majors. For this reason most tournament players use such overcalls conventionally, indicating two- or three-suiters of some sort.

This is the most popular scheme:

2♣ shows a two-suiter including hearts.
2◇ shows a two-suiter including spades.

When you are 5–4 in the majors you make the call that

indicates the five-card suit. With 5–5 in the majors you begin with 2♣.

The convention is easy to use.

(7)　♠ 9 6　♡ A Q 5 3　♢ A Q 10 6 2　♣ 6 3

You overcall 2♣, showing hearts and another. Partner will respond 2♡ with a moderate hand including at least three hearts. If instead he bids 2♢, denying three hearts but showing at least three diamonds, you will pass.

(8)　♠ A J 9 6 2　♡ 8 2　♢ A 6　♣ K Q 10 3

Here you bid 2♢, showing spades and another. If partner responds 2♡, you go to 2♠ to indicate your 5-card suit.

Bidding by fourth hand after the response to 1 NT

When the responder to 1 NT bids Stayman, or makes some potentially weak call at the two-level, the fourth player will often want to enter the auction. It is best to play that all doubles by the fourth player mean that he would have doubled 1 NT if this had come round to him.

(9)　♠ K Q 10 8　♡ A 7　♢ A Q 10 7 6　♣ Q 5

After 1 NT–Pass–2♣, or 1 NT–Pass–2♢ or 2♡ (whether or not the response was a transfer), you show your strength with a double. Make ♡A into a small heart and you would bid just 2♢, natural, over 2♣.

Bidding over a strong notrump

The general advice here is: Don't! In particular, it is silly to double a strong 1 NT just because you hold a scattered 17 points or so. It is much harder to defend when all your side's strength is in one hand. Also you can be fairly sure that there is no game your way.

1-star convention: two-suited double of 1 NT

Since there is little profit to be gained from a penalty double of a strong notrump, many tournament players use the bid to show either a major or a minor two-suiter. Partner will normally respond in his better minor, expecting you to transfer to 2♡ when you hold the majors.

The same convention may be used when a passed hand doubles a weak notrump. This often leads to an unexpected windfall when partner can leave in the double.

West
♠ K Q 10 5 4
♡ A J 8 3
♢ 8 2
♣ 10 5

West	*North*	*East*	*South*
Pass	1 NT[1]	Pass	Pass
?			

[1] 12–14 points.

West competes with a passed-hand double, in this case based on a major two-suiter. Such a call should guarantee at least 10 points; should he find East with a chunky 13–count, a useful 500 can be conjured out of thin air. When East is less well endowed he will pull the double to his longer minor and West, in this case, will bid 2♡.

19

Defence to Pre-empts

Conventional defences against opening three-bids come and go. At present in the tournament world there is an almost total reversion to take-out doubles. This is the most effective start to any auction over an enemy pre-empt, since it wastes no space. The only defect is that you lose the chance to make a penalty double, but quite often partner will volunteer a double in the fourth position.

In the second seat you may make a take-out double on about a king more than you would need for such a double at the one level.

    (1)   ♠ K Q 10 2   ♡ 5   ◇ A Q 9 4 2   ♣ K 10 4

Over 3♡ on your right you can double, for take-out. Make the ♠Q a small one and the double would be borderline.

In the protective seat you may double on somewhat less.

    (2)   ♠ K J 9 4   ♡ Q 10 3   ◇ J 2   ♣ A J 8 5

After 3◇–Pass–Pass most players would risk a take-out double. A bit dangerous, yes; but it is just as dangerous to pass, only to find that you had a part-score or game your way.

Responding to a double of three

As you see from the preceding examples, partner is tentatively assuming that you have around 8 points when he enters with a double. It follows that you should not respond too aggressively if this is all you do hold.

(3) ♠ 9 8 2   ♡ A Q 8 3   ◇ J 3   ♣ J 9 7 6

After 3◇–Dble–Pass you should respond just 3♡. On most hands where 4♡ is on, partner will have enough to advance further himself. He will not expect you to be completely bereft.

Here you have somewhat more, enough to insist on a game:

(4) ♠ A 10 8 7   ♡ K J 8 3   ◇ J 7 4   ♣ J 3

After the same start 3◇–Dble–Pass you respond 4◇, a cue-bid in the enemy suit. You are just showing that game should be on somewhere.

Let's look at some complete auctions initiated by a three-bid followed by a double.

West	East
♠ A K Q J 10 6	♠ 2
♡ K Q 10 2	♡ A J 9 7 3
◇ 3	◇ A 8 4
♣ K 5	♣ 10 8 4 2

West	North	East	South
–	–	–	3◇
Dble	Pass	4♡	Pass
4NT	Pass	5♡	Pass
6♠	End		

West bids the slam in spades to protect his ♣K from the opening lead.

West	East
♠ A K 4 2	♠ Q 5
♡ A Q 10 8 4	♡ J 9 2
◇ A 5	◇ K 10 8 6 2
♣ 8 6	♣ J 7 5

West	North	East	South
–	–	–	3♣
Dble	Pass	3◇	Pass
3♡	Pass	4♡	End

East responds at the minimum level and West advances to another suit. This shows fair values and East judges that he has enough to raise.

Responding to an overcall

The same sort of criteria apply when you are responding to an overcall over a pre-empt. A motley 7 or 8 points does not necessarily justify a raise to game.

(5) ♠ 10 8 7   ♡ Q J 7 5   ◇ Q 5 4   ♣ K 10 6

If partner says 3♠ over an enemy 3◇ you are not worth a raise. Had he bid 3♡ instead, you might raise to four, but not with any great confidence.

Defence against weak twos

When the opponents open with a weak two, again the take-out double bears most of the burden in defence.

(6) ♠ 6   ♡ K Q 9 4   ◇ J 10 2   ♣ A Q 9 5 2

When 2♠ is opened on your right you double, intending to pass any response at the minimum level. As always, if partner has a good hand it is his responsibility to show it, with a jump response or a cue-bid in the opponent's suit.

Here is a complete auction starting with a take-out double of a weak two.

West	East
♠ J 5	♠ Q 9 4
♡ A J 8 3	♡ 9 2
◇ A K J 10 5	◇ Q 9 4
♣ A 3	♣ K 10 8 4 2

West	North	East	South
–	–	–	2♠
Dble	Pass	3♣	Pass
3◇	Pass	3 NT	End

East, with an undistinguished 7-count, contents himself with a response at the minimum level. When West suggests some extra values by bidding again, East places the partnership in the game zone and bids 3 NT.

1-star convention: Lebensohl responses to double of weak two

In an auction such as 2♠–Dble–Pass–3◇, the strength of the 3◇ bidder is very much undefined; he might have a 9-count, might have a yarborough. In the Lebensohl system of responses you bid 2 NT on most hands of around 0–7 points (unless a two-level suit response is possible). This is the complete scheme of responses:

2 NT	0–7 points, any shape.
3 new suit	8–10 points.
cue-bid or games	11+ points.

When you respond 2 NT the doubler is expected to bid 3♣ next, unless he has extra strength or a long suit of his own. You may now either pass or sign off in some other suit.

This type of Lebensohl is helpful on a hand such as:

West	East
♠ 6	♠ J 9 8
♡ A K 9 8 7	♡ 6 4
◇ A 10 3	◇ Q 8 7 6 2
♣ K J 9 3	♣ 10 6 2

West	North	East	South
–	–	–	2♠
Dble	Pass	2NT	Pass
3♣	Pass	3◇	End

East bids a Lebensohl 2NT, indicating a weak hand. West dutifully bids 3♣ and East continues to 3◇, indicating his best suit. West has no reason to bid on. If, playing the Lebensohl scheme, East had made the more encouraging response of an immediate 3◇, West would have been strong enough to advance to 3♡.

Defence to four-level pre-empts

Doubles against opening pre-empts at the four-level are often called 'optional doubles'. This means that they show high cards rather than tricks in the enemy suit, and partner must use his judgement whether to defend or play the hand somewhere.

A double of an opening 4♡ should contain some tolerance for a spade contract, nearly always at least 3 cards in spades. 4NT over 4♡ suggests good values in the minors.

A double of 4♠ is in principle for penalties. 4NT over 4♠ indicates a two-suiter; partner should respond in his lowest playable suit.

20

Judgement at High Levels

Your opponents, who have the balance of the points, have bid to 4♡. Your side has a spade fit and you have to judge whether or not to sacrifice in 4♠. How do you make the right decision?

The various forms of the game give rise to different considerations. We will look first at team play, then at pairs. The tactics at rubber bridge are similar to those at teams, although other variable factors such as the state of the rubber and the quality of the opposition must be taken into account.

In team play

These are the general principles to bear in mind:

(a) When there has been a fair amount of bidding don't aim to make small gains – conceding 300 to save 420, 500 to save 620. Opponents will know where they stand and will double rather than bid one more. Occasionally you will find that you might have defeated them in their game contract.

(b) The best time to compete dangerously is when opponents have not had a lot of space in which to assess their combined strength. For example, at love all the bidding goes:

West	North	East	South
1♡	1♠	4♡	4♠

If West has a shapely hand, 1–6–4–2 or similar, he may go on when his partner was waiting to double. Then South, who has overbid, may end with a plus score.

(c) Most players are familiar with the techniques of the advance sacrifice, which arises in a sequence such as:

West	North	East	South
1♡	2◇	3♡	5◇
?			

Here South's jump to 5◇ is almost certainly an overbid and an attempt to disconcert the opposition. When West's next action is not clear-cut he can safely pass, confident that his partner will either double or battle on to 5♡. This manœuvre, known as a 'forcing pass', may be used whenever the opponents are clearly sacrificing.

It's time to look at a particular example.

> *South*
> ♠ K 10 8 7
> ♡ 5 4
> ◇ A Q 8 2
> ♣ J 8 5

East–West game

West	North	East	South
1♡	1♠	4♡	?

How many tricks would you expect to make in spades? You can't be precise, obviously. If partner has a minimum overcall and the hands don't fit well, you might end with only 7 tricks, but 8 or 9 is a more reasonable estimate.

How many tricks would you expect to make against 4♡? Probably not enough, though you might manage it if partner began with the ◇J through dummy's K.

At any rate, there is no doubt that with the vulnerability in his favour any experienced tournament player would bid 4♠. It won't cost a lot and you might get a brilliant result, your side having a fine fit in diamonds and the opponents a fit in clubs, which they haven't had time to discover.

At love-all or game-all the sacrifice is less attractive but still eminently worthwhile. Vulnerable against not? Now it is much closer. You might think it was a non-starter, risking 500 against an uncertain 420, but remember that your partner's overcall is now likely to be stronger. Also, the opponents are more likely to bid one more themselves, rather than risk suffering a 620. So, it's close but we would be there with 4♠.

This is a slightly different situation:

West
♠ A Q 10 5 4
♡ 8 4
◇ K Q 7
♣ Q 10 2

North–South game

West	*North*	*East*	*South*
1♠	2♡	2♠	4♡
?			

You may think that 4♠ will cost around 300 and there is no reason to expect 4♡ to fail. Why try to guess what partner's hand is like, though? It may be suitable for defending. There's nothing about your hand to incline you one way or the other and you should therefore pass, leaving the decision to partner.

Sacrificing at slam level

Slam sacrifices in IMP events are a less attractive proposition than most players think. The possible situations are infinite, but let's imagine that with neither side vulnerable South must find a call here:

	South		
	♠ Q 10 8 6		
	♡ 7 4		
	◇ K 9 6 5 2		
	♣ J 5		

West	North	East	South
1♡	1♠	2♣	2♠
3♣	Pass	4♡	Pass
4 NT	Pass	5◇	Pass
6♡	Pass	Pass	?

At love-all you may think of a sacrifice. Six spades is likely to go for 800 and if your other pair bid and make six hearts the gain will be 5 IMPs. Even if your other pair miss the slam, you will still save 3 IMPs by restricting the loss to 800 (instead of 980) in your room.

What if 6♡ would have failed, though? Now a sacrifice will be a disaster. Suppose your team-mates bid the heart slam and go one down; your sacrifice will cost 13 IMPs. Even worse, suppose your team-mates stop short, collecting 450. A sacrifice would now swap an 11-IMP gain for an 8-IMP loss.

Everything therefore depends on whether the enemy slam will make and it is easy to misjudge in this area. For example, your uninspiring ♣ J x may be facing ♣ Q x x in partner's hand. Even a dubious value like Q x under an opponent's long suit may yield a trick. Suppose the distribution is . . .

K J 10

9 x x   Q x

A 8 x x x

. . . your queen will probably live.

Conclusion: don't be smart in this area, sacrificing too often. It may look as though they are going to make their slam, but tricks sometimes arrive in funny ways.

High-level judgement at pairs

We are in a different world now. You have to play for small gains, despite the risk that (on a single board) you may have an expensive failure.

In IMP play, as we have noted, it is a mistake to invite a loss of 500 to save a vulnerable game that the opponents are not certain to make. In pairs play you have to do this sort of thing all the time. Quite often the opponents will go one higher in preference to doubling for a penalty that won't give them a good score. Everything is more tense.

Look at this type of auction:

East–West game

West	North	East	South
1♡	1♠	4♡	4♠
?			

Suppose West judges that he will take 500 against 4♠. At IMPs the double would be automatic. In pairs West may visualize other East-Wests registering 620 or 650. He must therefore seriously consider his chances of landing 5♡. At this stage in the auction he has three options available to him:

5♡   shows extra playing strength and a good expectation of eleven tricks;

Dble   shows a strong preference for defending;

Pass   is in effect forcing (since −420 can scarcely be a good board for his side); it invites partner to bid on, otherwise to double.

West might hold one of these hands:

(1)   ♠ 5   ♡ A Q 10 9 8 2   ◇ A J 7 4   ♣ K 2

With playing strength to spare, West would advance to 5♡.

(2)   ♠ 8 3   ♡ A K J 5 4   ◇ Q 10 2   ♣ K Q 6

Here West's hand is oriented towards defence. He would double.

(3) ♠ 10 9   ♡ K Q J 10 5 3   ◇ 8   ♣ A Q J 3

On this hand the right decision may depend on how many spades lie opposite. West passes, a forcing pass, leaving the decision to his partner.

Similarly, at slam level, the considerations are different from those at IMPs. Think back to the example we discussed above, where West held

(4) ♠ Q 10 8 6   ♡ 7 4   ◇ K 9 6 5 2   ♣ J 5

and had to consider a sacrifice in 6♠ over the opponents' 6♡. At IMPs we decided against the sacrifice, partly because the gain would be small, partly because a 'wrong view' would be very expensive. Neither of these considerations would have the same force at pairs. Small gains have almost the same worth as big gains. If you do the wrong thing it's only one board and the same may happen at other tables.

In a pairs you must calculate how many times the slam will be bid and made. It's not much use saving for 800 (or even 500) when the other pairs in your direction are conceding only 450 or 480. If you judge that the slam will not be widely bid, it is best to take your chance on defeating it. On the auction we gave previously it seemed likely that the slam would be widely bid. The sacrifice would therefore get our vote.

A final *caveat*: in the higher ranks of play you will find the odd crook who likes to bid vulnerable slams with two top losers in the enemy suit, hoping to draw you into a phantom sacrifice. How can you tell? Does the villain twitch his left eye or finger his gold ring?

Unfortunately not. Bridge can be a difficult game at times.